RECKLESSLY
IN *Love* WITH A
B-MORE
Thug

A NOVEL BY

BRIA S.

DEDICATION

This book is dedicated to any woman that has been through the struggle of giving their all in a relationship and was never able to receive back what they truly deserved. At one point in my life, I thought it was important for me to fall for that "perfect love." God allowed for the love of my life to continuously reveal his evil ways, leaving me no choice but to give up on him. Eventually it made me realize that we can fall deeply in love with people who aren't meant to be a part of our forever. People can be our soul mates without it lasting forever. We tend to want to believe, just because we are deep in love with a person, we have to spend eternity with them. When in reality, we fall in love with certain individuals to learn life lessons. And it's meant for us to use those lessons in order to turn them into our footstools, in order to push us into our purpose and destiny. Sometimes we fear that we will create mistakes and regrets by giving up early on a person. We have to realize it's not necessarily a mistake, but it is a part of the blessing to come. Dragging out a relationship will only further block our own blessing. Sometimes we fear being alone, so we push for love and fulfillment through others. Filling our own voids through others is dangerous. God made us to be rightfully one in our own. How can you ever be whole living your best life through someone else? You have to love yourself 100 percent before you can love anyone else. If you don't, you run the risk of developing a spirit of using and leeching because you haven't fully loved yourself in order to fully come correct to the next person. Why allow yourself to consistently live in falsehood? We should all strive to be in healthy relationships. In a real healthy and well-balanced relationship, you will never have to guess your position in a person's life. You will be at peace and live in wholeness. God Bless!

Author Bria S.

CHAPTER 1

Logan

I swear I was sick of this damn night shift shit. God bless the women who did for themselves, but damn. I was really worn out. I'm Logan. Everybody calls me Lo or Lo Lo. I'm twenty-three and work at University of Maryland Hospital as an ER trauma RN, in downtown Baltimore, but my true passion is cooking. Ever since my mom first taught me how to boil an egg at five years old, it had been on for me in the kitchen ever since.

On my 7 a.m. ride home, I could do nothing but deeply think about my dreams and aspirations of eventually opening a restaurant and being a top well-known chef, but my controlling ass father that I loved dearly didn't feel that being a chef was a real solid career choice, especially since he was funding my college education throughout school.

I was secretly an heiress to one of Baltimore's biggest drug kingpins that was able to make it out of the game without being dead or in jail. Big Rell and Shontrice Brown were my parents. My mom has never really had to work since they've been together. She opened a clothing boutique to keep herself busy from being home all day and bored, but she always pushed me to do for me, to be more independent than she was, and not to wait on a man to live off of.

My phone ringing interrupted my thoughts. I glanced down at my phone and saw it was Shay, my brother's on and off girlfriend and baby mama. I slightly rolled my eyes, wondering what the fuck she could want this early.

"Hello," I said dryly. Instead of Shay's voice, I heard a squeaky little voice.

"Auntie! I'm getting ready to go to daycare. I just wanted to call to tell you I love you!"

"Aww! Thanks, Ken Ken. I love you too! Be a good girl today at daycare. Where's your mom?"

"She's in the bathroom, brushing her teeth."

"Okay, well finish getting yourself ready, and put your mommy's phone back on the charger. I will see you later when I pick you up from daycare."

"Okay, Auntie. See you later!" Click.

I laughed to myself at how smart and attentive Kennedy was. She may have been my niece, but that little four-year-old was the light of my life. She'd been glued to my hip since she was able to walk. She even had her own room at my condo. My older brother, Brandon, and Shay had been together on and off since they were in high school. They were the epitome of your average hood couple… you know… the fights, the make up to break ups, and the hustler and wife combo. Brandon was always smart and talented. Compared to his friends, he always made decent grades and was a football star athlete, but I guess reality took over after college for him. He decided to follow in our father's footsteps and eventually took over the family's drug empire when our dad, Big Rell, was the king of Baltimore and decided to settle in retirement.

Between my dad being who he was and my brother taking after his footsteps, I was very sheltered, especially when it came to dating as a teen. They wouldn't keep me out of their eyesight and control. My mother would complain but was always quickly shut down because Big Rell didn't play about his one and only baby girl. While I was in college at Morgan State, I was able to finally gain some freedom and began exploring into the boy world.

By the time I graduated earlier this year, I wasn't too beat for the love department anymore. I'd had my fun, but I was a young woman focused on my cash and making a name for myself in this crazy world. The last nigga I met had invited me out on a date, and when the check came, he asked for the bill to be split. The next day, he had the nerve to ask if he could move in with me, so at this point, fuck the fuckboys! I would just continue on my independent woman spree for now. Plus, my brother would literally kill any nigga that came to me incorrectly, and he definitely wouldn't think twice about it!

I pulled up to my condo complex that was located downtown in the Federal Hill area, a few blocks away from the Inner Harbor, and I barely could get out of my car. My feet felt like a ton of bricks were weighing me down. My body was beat from standing ten hours straight during my shift. Before lying down, I decided to call my bestie, Quinn. I knew she was up early. Today was her birthday, so she was having a big party tonight. It was definitely going to be an event for anybody that was somebody in Baltimore tonight. As soon as she said hello, I screamed in my best thot voice.

"HAPPY BIRTHDAY, BIIIIIITCH!"

She giggled a bit.

"THANKS, BESTFRIEEEEND!"

"Quinn, I hope you really ready for tonight. We are about to shut shit down."

"I know. I'm actually on my way to pick up the Bentley that I rented for us to ride out in tonight!"

"Oh my God. No, Quinn. That was supposed to be my gift for you. I was gonna pick it up and pay for it."

"I know, but I just went ahead and got it. I knew you would be tired from working all night. Besides, my lil' African I've been dealing with lately footed the bill."

I laughed.

"Ugh! Girl, I don't see how you can deal with that type. He's damn near fifty, and you can barely understand anything he says."

Quinn busted out laughing.

"Girl, you know I don't take none of these fools seriously. I get what I want and then dip."

I laughed again.

"Girl, you are a trip."

"Lo, I'm finding you some dick tonight. It's been way overdue for you."

"Oh Lorrrddd, Quinn. Please! You know I'm on a hiatus right now, ever since I stopped dealing with Trent's ol' ignorant ass. I just want to refocus on building my life and career."

"Blah, blah, blah, girl. Whatever. I'ma find you a man, whether you like it or not... end of discussion, bye. I gotta go. Call me when you wake up this afternoon."

When I got up a few hours later, I knew it was time to get Kennedy from daycare. I got in the car and realized I needed gas of course. I pulled up to the gas station not far from my house. As I was pulling in, I spotted a familiar car, a black on black Mercedes S550. It belonged to my brother's best friend, Deandre, better known as Dre on the streets. Dre and Brandon had been thick as thieves for years, so it was only right when my father passed down the family business to Brandon that he made Dre his right-hand man.

I hoped like hell Dre didn't spot me pull up. He'd had a crush on me for years. Dre was a man whore, and I never wanted any parts of him. On top of that, Brandon would off the both of us if we ever fooled around.

I stepped into the store, and I didn't see Dre anywhere in sight. *Good. He must have not seen me and pulled off,* I thought to myself. I went over to the freezer to get me and Kennedy something to drink, since she always complained about how thirsty she was every time I picked her up. Next thing I knew, I felt a hand slowly slide up and down against my thigh and heard a deep voice whisper, "When you gonna stop playing and let me have you, Lola Bunny?"

Next thing you know, the steam had risen throughout my body. Did I mention that I was overall naturally curvy? Yes, I was team thick at a size twelve pants and about a size medium top, so when my body temp rose, it really rose! I felt the beads of sweat forming on my forehead. I flinched and backed up quickly, almost slapping his ass with my quick reflexes. I may have been able to grow up fortunate, but that didn't mean I wasn't quick to throw hands, and I knew how to use them.

"Dre, what the fuck? I was about to haul off and rock ya ass up. Stop playing with me! You of all people should know better than to run up on somebody like that!" I yelled and playfully nudged his shoulder as he started dying laughing.

"Damn, Lo Lo. It's like that? I thought you was gonna be happy to see daddy."

"Dre, shut up."

I started walking toward the cash register, doing my best to avoid him. Of course, Dre started following right behind me, damn near on my heels.

"Let me get twenty dollars on seven and these two Sprites."

As the cashier said my total, Dre threw down a hundred-dollar bill on the counter.

"What's that for, Dre?"

"Don't worry about it, baby mama. I got you. It's more of that to come and keep the change. Get yourself something to eat."

"What you mean *baby mama*?"

"Exactly what it sounds like, Lo," Dre said, staring me straight in the eyes. I was a bit taken aback, but I had to keep my composure like it didn't faze me. A nigga like him would take full advantage if I began to look flustered. Next thing I knew, my forehead started sweating, and my underwear got soaked. *I gotta get the fuck out of this place! Shit!*

"Thanks, Dre. I gotta run."

I quickly pushed my way out of the store and went to grab the pump to pump my gas, but Dre walked up quickly, grabbed it out my hand, and began pumping it for me.

"Ain't no lady of mine gonna be pumping her own gas," Dre said.

"I'm far from being your lady, Dre. You are somet—"

Before I could finish my sentence, I heard a ghetto ass female's voice screaming from Dre's passenger side window.

"DRE, HOW THE FUCK YOU GONNA BE ALL IN ANOTHER BITCH FACE WHILE I'M IN YOUR CAR?"

I shook my head.

"You love them hood rats, don't you? You better go handle her before I do."

"Man, that lil' whore is just something to do. I will see you at the party tonight though."

"How do you know about my best friend's party?" I asked matter-of-factly.

"I know everything, baby."

Dre blew a kiss at me and walked backward to his car. I smiled, shaking my head and then hopped back in my car, pulling off in the direction of Kennedy's daycare. A few minutes later, I pulled up. Before I could get my foot all the way in the door, Kennedy was running toward me.

"Auntie! Auntie!"

"Hey, Ken Ken. Have you been a good girl today?"

"Yesssss!" she dramatically squealed. I went to sign Kennedy out and noticed my phone ringing. It was Brandon, probably wondering if I had picked Kennedy up yet.

"What's up, sis?"

"Nothing. Just picked Ken Ken up."

"Daddyyyyy!" Kennedy interrupted.

"My lil' princess! What you doing? How was school?"

"Goooood! I got all five stars today, Daddy. I was really good. Where are you, Daddy?"

"Aw, baby girl, I'm handling business right now, but I will make sure I come get you from Auntie's house. Okay?"

"Okay! Love you, Daddy!" Click! Kennedy had a tendency to not say bye when being on the phone with people. We were all working on her with that.

"Ken, you have to say bye before you hang up the phone, munchkin. It's rude."

"I forgooooot. Tell Daddy I sorry."

Ken was so dramatic. I texted Brandon.

Me: Your child said she was sorry she forgot to say bye.

Brandon: Lol I already knew.

Me: Please come get her by seven, u know I gotta do a lot to get ready for the party.

Brandon: Damn! Chill Lo Lo! I got this lol

Me: And I expect my weekly gas money in hand as well when you come. Please and thank you.

*Brandon: *middle finger**

We got back to my house, and I made Kennedy a small meal to hold her over until she ate dinner at home. I got her situated to watch cartoons as I began the process of doing my hair. Of course, I got the draining bright idea to sew in my own hair. My usual hairstylist was unfortunately booked until next week.

Brandon

I pulled up to my sister's house. I had just hung up the phone from arguing with my pops Big Rell about some lil' niggas I let do some runs for me outta town. Big Rell didn't like new faces. The way I looked at it was if you crossed this operation, you signed your own death certificate. If I found a new employee every now and then, I didn't see anything wrong with it. He was retired, but if you let that nigga tell it, he was still tryna run the operation. I always had to reinforce and remind him that the game had changed. I'd been in charge a little over four years now, and of course I ran a tight ship. My crew and I supplied the dope in this city from east to west and north to south. Any nigga in Baltimore knew who the fuck Brandon a.k.a B-Mac was, and if they didn't know me, they knew who my pops was. Running an operation worth millions wasn't easy, but I knew what I was doing.

I knocked on the door, and I could hear Kennedy running to the door at a hundred miles per hour. Even though I was tough as nails, my baby girl had the softest place in my heart.

"What's going on, my lil' princess?"

I picked her up and gave her a kiss on the cheek. I was a firm believer in setting an example of fathers being their daughter's first example of healthy love. I was a street nigga with logic. I'd be damned if my daughter grew up not knowing the right way to be treated by a man. Of course I was going to set the standard.

"Lo Lo! What's up, sis!" I yelled out. Logan came from her room.

"Bro bro, what it do? You got my money, nigga?"

I laughed and passed her a stack of money.

"You terrible, Logan. Ain't I supposed to be the big brother?"

"It's all business, shorty," she said, tryna mock me. I sat down on the couch.

"Yo, your father is trippin' though. He keeps tryna tell me how to run shit like I'm not my own man or something."

"Brandon, come on. You know how Daddy is. He's so used to pointing the finger, that he doesn't really understand falling back. You gotta give him some time, big bro."

"You know I'm stubborn just like him, Lo."

She laughed.

"Yeah, I know. Maybe we could get Ma to talk to him. You never tried that."

I sat in silence for a second.

"Man, I don't think that would work, but you know I'ma nigga that doesn't like to try and complain about too much. I just deal with shit and keep moving."

I got up and gathered up Kennedy's stuff.

"Ard, sis. See you tonight. Love ya."

"Love ya, bro."

On the ride home, I got a call from my boy, Dominic aka Dom.

He and Dre were the heads of my trap houses.

"Yo, yo, what's good, nigga?"

"Man, I can't complain. What that money looking like tonight?"

"You know everything looking good. I had to holla at lil' Man Man about posting shit on Instagram. It's way too many FEDS on there."

I looked in the rearview at Kennedy, knocked out sleep. I didn't like talking business around her.

"Hell yeah. He knows better. If he does it again, send his ass straight to me. But aye, is you and my sis, Malia, coming through tonight?"

"Most definitely. I'll see you then."

"You already know! Tonight finna be an all-white movie."

"Hell yeah. Aight, nigga."

I got home, hoping that Shay had cooked. We had been high school sweethearts, so of course we had an off and on relationship the past few years, with me being in the streets and messing around with different bitches. All that changed when Kennedy came along. I guess maturity set in. I had given her a ring and everything. Even though we hadn't gotten to the altar yet, she always promised me she would remain a hustler's wife. I had pulled up to the house. Kennedy was still knocked out, leaving me no choice but to carry her in the house, along with juggling the bags she insisted on bringing with her to school every day.

I had to start getting ready for the party. Shay's younger sister, Kiara, was coming over to watch Kennedy while we went to the party. Shay didn't trust me going to the party by myself, because she knew the history between me and Quinn. Years ago, Lo tried setting us up together while Shay and I were on one of our lil' breaks. Lo and Shay's relationship had never been the strongest to begin with. I guess not too many sisters liked their brother's significant others. Shay saw me struggling, trying to get in the door with Kennedy in my arms, so she lightly grabbed Ken to take her upstairs in her room. I walked in the kitchen, and my phone began to ring. It was my nigga, Dre's, crazy ass.

"Yoooo, what's good, nigga," I said.

"Ain't shit. I can't call it. But look, I wanted to holla at you about something tonight, man to man."

"Business or personal?" I asked with a concerned tone.

Dre chuckled. "Calm down, nigga. It's some personal shit I wanna run by you. You know business is always smooth on my end."

I breathed smoothly. "Oh, alright. Man, you almost had me shook there for a minute. I talked to my pops earlier, and he had me heated, still tryna run shit and fussing about our new runners. You know I'm a paranoid type of nigga. I don't be liking to hear all of that negativity. Negative vibes bring too much negative energy. We already ducking and dodging the FEDS as it is. Every other week, he is calling me on the same bull."

"Yeah, he do. Man, maybe we gotta have a meeting or some type of sit down with ya pops, man. It's like he trusted you enough to pass down the empire with the connects and all, but he still wants to have some type of control. All he has to do is sit back and enjoy his retirement with his feet up and blow the Hydro in the air every day." Dre and I laughed a bit.

I felt Shay come up and hug me from behind.

"Aye, Dre. I will see you later tonight. Hit my phone when you leaving out."

I hung up, turned her around, and pulled her in close to me.

"So you really stepping out with me tonight?" I asked Shay.

"You know I'm coming. I know you tryna support 'family' and all, but technically, Quinn ain't really family, and given the history between y'all two, you know I definitely don't trust y'all nowhere near each other, especially if I'm not around."

"Come on now, Shay. Stop bringing shit up from years ago. Didn't we agree we were gonna let it go."

Got damn! A nigga can't catch a break today. Yeah, me and Quinn fucked around for about a month a few years ago, but we both moved on, point blank. I shook my head, stepping away from her.

"Man, I'm about to go lie down and take a nap. My damn head hurt. Wake me up at eleven so I can get dressed." Shay just shook her head and let out a deep sigh. I just kept having this feeling that something bad was about to happen. All this extra negativity had to end.

CHAPTER 2

Dre

I had just gotten back in the house from being in the street all day, overseeing shit. I kicked my sneakers off and sat on the couch with my eyes closed and my head leaned back. I had damn near kicked Shanika's loud ass out the car. I let her top me off when I pulled up to her house, and then I lied and told her I had some other business to handle. She begged for me to pick her up today so that she could ride around with me. Shorty was just something to do. She barely had a job and had nothing to show for herself.

In the meantime, I wanted out of this damn fake ass relationship with Candi, my live-in girlfriend. She was a stripper at Stadium Club in D.C. When we first met, shit was cool. I was just coming home from doing a year in jail, and she was just getting her feet wet in the strip club scene. I couldn't say it was love at first sight, but she was definitely a hustler, and that was about the only thing I respected about her, honestly. My mama couldn't stand her. She didn't even know we lived together. Shit, nobody knew, not even Brandon. I was always at his house. That was how much of a secret I kept her in my life. My mama always repeated that you couldn't turn a hoe into a housewife. She always wanted for me to pursue Logan, but a couple months into me and Candi hanging out, we somehow decided to move in together.

Two years later, I could honestly say that was one of the worst decisions I'd ever made. I guess I was a nigga fresh outta jail and scared of not having any type of stability. I'd had my eyes on Logan since we were kids. Lo may have been on the thick side, but she was still A1. Besides, I loved the fact she had her own everything. She wasn't the type that was looking in a nigga's pockets all the time, like most of the bitches I fucked with.

I used to be boiling on the inside when Brandon would tell me the crazy shit she was dealing with when she called herself being with that clown ass nigga, Trent. It was a few times I had to stop myself from randomly sneaking up and knocking that nigga off myself after certain shit I heard he had done to Logan. Of course, out of respect for my man Brandon and his family, I always knew she was off limits, so I kept my distance. Lately, it was becoming a lot tougher for me to keep my distance though. I dealt with so many different bitches over the years that I couldn't keep up, but for some reason, I always compared them to Logan, especially comparing her and Candi.

I knew Lo understood and respected the lifestyle. Hell, she was raised in it. A street nigga like me needed a solid lady by his side to keep him afloat. His mom and pops were like my second family. Most of everything I knew about the streets and handling business I learned from Big Rell. He and my dad, Kevin, were close back in the day, but after he was killed, I guess he figured it was his responsibility to step up to the plate in honor of my dad being gone. When my dad died, I was ten years old. My mom, Pam, and I were pretty much left assed out.

My parents weren't good at the time with saving money. My father made thousands in a week's time doing business with Big Rell, but them being young and dumb at the time, they would spend the money as soon as they would get it on cars, clothes, expensive vacations, you name it. There were many days I spent with Brandon and the family while my mom was forced to get a real job at the time in order to make ends meet. It hurt like hell having to watch my mom struggle with depression and doing the best she could to keep up and make ends meet, and she always refused the money Big Rell and Shontrice offered. I had made it my business to take care of her as I got older. As soon as I made my first 100K, I moved her back to a good neighborhood in a luxury townhouse and copped her a white BMW X6.

"Deandre!" Candi yelled from behind me, breaking my thoughts.

"What, Candi? Damn." I jumped up.

"Well hello to you too, Dre! I've been calling your damn phone all day, and you've obviously been ignoring me," Candi stated, putting her hands on her hips.

"Man, go 'head with that. You know I'm in the streets all day, getting money. I left my phone in the car. You don't be complaining when I hand you stacks of cash, or when I bought you that G-Wagon last month."

She rolled her eyes. "Why do we always have to keep having this same argument? Sometimes, I'm just concerned for your well-being out there. We all know the murder rate in Baltimore is sky high."

"Candi, just leave it alone. Don't you gotta go shake your ass tonight at work? Go get some rest instead of worrying about me." I got up, leaving her standing there. I went upstairs to hop in the shower so that I could get dressed. I would just go to Brandon's house and pre-game so that I could get away from Candi quicker. She hated when I went out. I could admit I was a bit immature at times. Instead of me telling her how I really felt, I would just avoid her at all cost. But shit, I was more than positive she was tricking off after she was done climbing the pole. We hadn't had sex in months, and I wasn't bothered by far. I had a rack of other bitches, but Candi was the only one I could depend on for now.

***

I pulled up to Dre's house, and Shay opened the door for me.

"What's up, sis?" I asked.

"Damn, Dre. You by yourself tonight? You never roll out alone. You always gotta girl with you," she joked.

"Nah, I'ma be the third wheel and ride along with y'all tonight."

"Uncle Dre!" Kennedy yelled, running down the steps.

"Ken Ken, what's happening, baby girl?"

I picked her up and playfully threw her in the air while she started giggling.

"Can you come to my dance recital next month? You never came before," Ken Ken asked, staring me directly in my eyes. Shay started laughing. *Now what does my hood nigga looking ass look like coming in a little prissy ass dance recital? I'm a tall ass chocolate nigga with golds in my mouth, but I can't tell my lil' goddaughter no to her face.*

"How about you take this twenty dollars, put it in your piggy bank, and I will look at my schedule and see if I can make it, baby girl."

The entire time, Shay was cracking up at how uneasy I looked. Kennedy took the twenty dollars and went in the living room to watch TV with Kiara. Brandon came down the stairs with a bottle of Hennessy in his hand. We took some shots, and a few minutes later, we hopped in Brandon's all-black Maserati Quattroporte. I got in the back seat.

On our way downtown, I lit my blunt that I had pre-rolled, took a few pulls, and passed it up to the front. Usually when I went out, I was a lot more amped-up. I had Logan still on my brain from seeing her earlier. It wasn't too often I was able to see her, let alone by herself. Now I was a boss type nigga, so me lusting over a female for a long period of time was way out of my character. I could have any chick I wanted, but I had to have her. I had to grow some balls and approach my bro Brandon about it, tonight. It was only right. We'd known each other too long to all of a sudden have bad blood between one another, especially with the type of business we were into.

Logan

I had finally finished my hair and began doing my makeup when Quinn texted me, letting me know she was on her way over. I had Cardi B's "Bartier Cardi" blasting in the background. I was so pumped for tonight. I was the type of friend that got more wasted than the actual friend whose birthday it actually was. When I was done, I put on an all-white one-shoulder bodycon dress with my nude So Kate Christian Louboutins. I heard my doorbell ring. When I opened the door, Quinn came blasting in my condo with a huge gallon bottle of Patron in hand.

"Okay, birthday girl! I see how you tryna act tonight. This bedazzled bodysuit you got on is definitely gonna stop traffic tonight. Bitch, look at that ass!"

Quinn was a mixed girl. Her mama was Italian, and her daddy was Black. Baby girl was about a size eight but definitely had curves and long beautiful black curly hair. She and I had been rocking since ninth grade. We had both attended Western High School, an all-girls school in North Baltimore. At first, I hated the idea of my parents making me go to an all girl's school, but as soon as Quinn and I connected there, we were unstoppable. She was pretty much the only female I trusted. We had been there for one another through the make ups and break ups over trifling niggas, getting by in college, and fighting hating bitches. You name it.

"Lo, are you gonna hit this blunt with me tonight, or what?" Quinn asked, sitting on the couch and lighting up. Quinn was usually the party girl with the big mouth and personality to match. I liked to turn up, but I was a bit more reserved. I think it had a lot to do with how I was raised in a low-key environment because of my father's empire.

"Now, girl, you know I don't mess with that stuff. You know I am a true drinker. Pop that bottle open. I need to relieve some stress. Work has been so tiring this week. I wanna get so drunk that I gotta hold the grass in order to get up."

We both cracked up laughing. We took two shots. I went in my room to get her gift. It was the same red Caviar Shoulder Chanel bag that I knew she had been wanting.

"Oh my gosh, Logan. No you didn't! You knew I've been wanting this bag but couldn't afford it! You are the bestest bestest friend ever!" Quinn screamed dramatically.

"Girl, calm down. You're welcome! Come on. Let's get out of here and turn up." Quinn quickly transferred everything she had in her previous bag she had on into the new one. I laughed at her so hard. We walked outside. I saw the red Bentley she'd rented and got even more excited. I had to catch myself from tripping on the curb. Those two shots had snuck up on me quick.

"Bitch, watch yourself. Don't start already!" Quinn yelled at me.

I laughed. It wasn't too often that I got to let loose with my busy work schedule. We got in and Quinn started blasting Lil' Baby's song, "My Dawg".

Yeah that's my dawg for sure

Yeah that's my dawg

Yeah that's my dawg for sure

Yeah that's my dawg

We began rapping out loud, making videos, and taking pictures for Snapchat and Instagram.

"Girl, you better slow down before we get pulled over with all this liquor we got in the car."

"Lo, chill. I got this. It's my night. Stop being so paranoid." She tried to hush me.

"You're right, but still…"

She turned the music back up even louder and ignored me. Since I already lived downtown, it didn't take long for us to pull up. I texted Brandon.

Me: Wya

Brandon: We'll be there in about 10 min

Me: Cool we are pulling up now, the VIP section is under Quinn name

Brandon: Ard bet

When we pulled up to the valet, it was definitely all eyes on us. Everybody in line was tryna see who was pulling up in this brand new red Bentley. Quinn's Italian uncle on her mom's side owned the club, so of course we walked up and went directly in. The club was already lit. He had the decorations already set, and a few bottles of Rosé were coming our way as soon as we stepped foot in the section. I spotted my co-worker, Kelsi, in the crowd and dragged her along with us. She'd hung out with us a while back.

"Kelz, what are you doing in here by yourself? I could never step out by myself!" I yelled over the music as we sat on the couch.

"You know I am not scared to mix and mingle alone, Lo. You need to do it more often, that way you can meet a man."

"Girl, bye. You know I'm not built for that."

I playfully waved her off and stood up to look over the balcony down at the crowd. *Speaking of which, I just remembered Dre said he would be coming tonight. I sure hope he doesn't show up.*

I was feeling a bit uneasy about our little encounter earlier. No matter what, I always looked at him like another brother. My panties actually got wet in the store. That was a no no for me. He had always given me the vibe like he had a crush on me, even as kids, but I had never paid him any mind just because of the family circumstances. Within the last two or three years, he'd started coming on to me in ways I'd never expected. I always just brushed him off without flirting back. Besides, he was a complete and absolute man whore, and I never wanted to entertain that type of man. That was the exact reason why Trent and I ended. I didn't care how overweight I ever was. I always had confidence, kept myself up, dressed well, and embraced who I was. I would never chase a man or entertain foolishness.

I felt a tap on my shoulder. It felt like I had a déjà vu moment, and I had just come back to my senses.

Quinn was staring at me, confused. "Bitch, did you forget it's my birthday? Wake up! Here. Take this cup, granny, and snap out of it. And you better down it. Drink every last drop." I rolled my eyes, taking the cup from her and chuckled.

"You're right. My fault."

We began to dance. The liquor completely helped me get out of my thoughts. Kodak Black's "Skrilla" was playing. I saw my brother walking up with Shay and Dre behind him. I had to prepare myself to be around not only Dre, but also Shay's bad energy that she always brought along with her. I'm sure the only reason she came was because she wanted to keep an eye on Brandon because of Quinn.

I greeted all of them with a hug, introduced Kelsi to them, and went back to dancing on the other side of the section, trying to avoid Dre by any means. A few of Quinn's cousins joined us in the section, so after a while, I asked Kelsi if she wanted to go on the dance floor to mingle a bit. She agreed.

"Lo, that Dre dude has been eyeing you since they got here," she leaned in to say.

"Yeah, I know. I'm tryna keep my distance from his ass. He's my brother's best friend." I looked annoyed.

"Damn. Well come on. Let's keep moving through the crowd so that we can dance in peace."

Dre

Logan is most certainly looking good tonight. She's mine, and she don't even know it. I was staring down on the dance floor, watching Logan's every move. Brandon crept up, standing next to me and leaning on the balcony.

"Aye, Dre. Man, you good? You acting real unusual, nigga. What the fuck is up? I know the bud and Henny ain't got you that throwed off," Brandon said, chuckling a little bit.

"Man, B-Mac, I need to holla at you about Logan. This shit has been on my mind for a minute now."

Brandon looked at me confused. I looked him straight in the eyes.

"Look… straight up, I want Logan to be my girl. I know it may sound crazy, coming from a thug nigga like me, and we like family, but that's more reason I wanted to come at you correctly about how I felt. That's what I was talking about earlier when I had called you."

Brandon paused for a minute, rubbing his chin. Meanwhile, I could feel Shay staring a hole into me while she was sitting on the couch, trying to figure out what we were talking about that was so serious.

"Listen, Dre. You know that's lil' sis, and me, nor Pops have ever played about her whatsoever!"

"I know, yo. It's all love and respect over here. I'm just tryna be a man about this shit. I just want your blessing on this, bro."

Brandon stared me dead in my eyes with no emotion.

"Give me some time to think about it, man. I'm not gonna be quick to say yes or no. I know what type of nigga you are when it comes to these women. You are gambling with your life trying to get at Logan! You sure you ready, nigga? Yo, Pops is going kill your ass once he finds this shit out, and you're gonna be the one to tell him, not me. All of y'all mafuckas around me are starting to stress me out."

Brandon shook his head. He was always trying to be the sensible one. I laughed at him. Dom and Malia had finally made it, and their entrance kind of interrupted our conversation. We greeted them both, and Malia went over to dance with Shay. Quinn and her cousins had joined Logan and Kelsi on the dance floor by this time. I had passed Dom one of the Hennessy bottles we had on the table, and I saw Brandon flagging the waitress girl down, trying to order more bottles. One thing about this crew was that when we went out, we always showed out, but we always stayed in VIP. We were too bossed up to mix and mingle in with the crowd.

A few minutes later, Logan and the girls came back in the section in order to rest their feet, I assumed. Of course, I still had eyes on her. I didn't care how wasted she looked. Brandon caught me a few times and kept shaking his head. I guess I gave that nigga the shock of a lifetime tonight because after our whole conversation, he was throwing the Henny back even more than usual. I wasn't a dancing type of nigga, but as I continued to stand on the balcony next to Dom, I noticed a few niggas from over east that we had been beefing with for months now over territory. They were hating off the fact that we were stealing clientele from them. Me being me, I confronted them a few weeks ago and pretty much told them to kiss our asses. If they wanted to get real money, they needed to join our team.

One of their lieutenants didn't take too kindly to what I had to say and called himself pulling out his gun on me, acting tough, and his faggot ass didn't even end up having any bullets in his piece. I straight up sent a message and aired his ass flat out in broad daylight on Monument Street, and I dared anybody to snitch on me. I was the most hot-headed one in our crew. I could remember offing a nigga just for looking at me too hard. Brandon, Dom, nor I had absolutely any patience for bullshit or anything that didn't go our way. We had a whole empire, legacy, and reputation to protect.

I leaned in a little closer to Dom and asked his opinion about the niggas to make sure it was them. By this time, YBS Skola's "Shinning" was blasting. Brandon must've gotten extra lit. He got up and started hitting his Baltimore two-step hard as shit. Shay looked around, embarrassed. Everybody else was pumping him up and recording him for Instagram or that Snapchat shit. People on the dance floor had begun to take notice, looking up at the balcony and trying to see Brandon go off. Usually, I would have joined in on the turn up, but right now, given the circumstances, it was not the time or place.

I guess the niggas downstairs must've caught on quick because next thing we knew, gunshots started firing in our direction from the dance floor. Lo and Quinn had been standing next to me, recording Brandon. With all my bodyweight, I pushed them down to the floor so that they wouldn't get hit. People started running like crazy, trying to get to the exit. B- Mac couldn't have been that tore up, because by the time I stood back up two seconds later, he had his tool out, shooting toward the entire dance floor. After pushing all the girls back, Dom and I joined in on the action with him. I had never seen so many people running that fast at one time in my damn life. Security came in like they were the military and bum rushed the crowd. From what I could tell, Brandon may have hit one of them niggas. I saw a body lying on the ground with blood pouring out. We couldn't afford to take a charge for a body at this point!

"We got to get the fuck out of here!" I yelled out.

"Let's go! Get the girls!" Dom yelled. Naturally, I rushed toward Logan and picked her up, trying to cover her body at the same time. She looked scared as shit. I began to feel a sense of guilt that I had never felt before, especially when a female was around. We all ran down the stairs toward the back-emergency exit. Everybody ran quick as hell to their individual cars. I got in the Bentley with Quinn and Lo and told Quinn to just follow Brandon. We saw the sirens headed in the direction of the club. I had to lean back and thank God that we were able to get out of there in time. Niggas couldn't afford to go back to jail any time soon.

We all got back to B-Mac's house and sat around in silence in the living room. The girls were still a bit shaken up. Quinn's cousins and Kelsi had called to let them know they were home safe.

𝓑𝓻𝓪𝓷𝓭𝓸𝓷

"Aye, Dom and Dre, let's chop it up in the basement real quick."

We all walked down into my theater room.

"I feel like I lost my head in there. I fucked up. You know I'm always the one to try to protect the family by any means. Getting drunk in the club wasn't a good look at all. I've been so stressed lately. I'm the one always trying to make sure everybody stays on point and well protected."

"Man, we all have our moments, B-Mac. We just got to lay low for a few days," said Dre.

"In the meantime, we gotta rethink some new shit and look into some new stash houses because you know them niggas will try to hit us up after all of this," Dom firmly stated.

"Yeah. You're right, Dom. But y'all go ahead and get home. I will hit y'all up in the morning so that we can link up. I need to lay back and think this shit over. And Dre, you got my permission to move forward. Don't fuck it up. I appreciate what you did for sis tonight. Don't fuck it up. That's ya head if you do!"

I looked him directly in the eyes. We all dapped each other up and walked back up the stairs.

"Aye, Lo. Dre is gonna take you home." She gave me a funny look.

"I rode with Quinn. She can take me home."

The whole room looked at Quinn, and she looked up at me. I gave her the eye to make sure she went along with what I was trying to do. Dom and Malia were leaving out the door while Dre stood there looking happy as hell. Quinn caught the hint.

"Nah, girl. Let Dre take you. I'm tired as hell, and I really just wanna go straight home and get in my bed after tonight's events."

She gave Lo a hug and said her goodbyes.

CHAPTER 3

Logan

I didn't know what type of shit my brother and Quinn were on, but at this point, all I wanted to do was go home as soon as possible. My heart felt like it was still trying to beat out of my damn chest from the club shooting. Now they sprung this shit on me. I had already been trying to avoid this nigga Dre all fucking night as it was, and got damn. Dre looked so fucking good tonight. As soon as he stepped in our VIP section, my thong got wet.

God, I pray I can keep my composure during this twenty-minute ride home.

I told everybody goodnight and walked out of the door before Dre could even get outside. I was standing at the passenger side door, waiting for him to come out, while flipping through my Instagram timeline. Dre had finally come outside a few moments later.

"Damn. My bad, Lo Lo. I didn't realize you were in that much of a rush. Step back. Let me be a gentleman and open the door for you."

"Thanks." I rolled my eyes and took a deep breath when I sat down.

He got in, and we started riding. He turned on some old Boosie. As we were riding, I noticed one of his phones kept flashing. He would look down at it and then silence the call. Yes, this nigga had an iPhone and two flip phones for business purposes. I already knew, and that was already strike fifty in my mind. I just sat back, vibing to Boosie's voice and staring out of the window, pretending that I could actually see out of this nigga's dark ass five percent tint. Out of the corner of my eye, I kept noticing him stealing glances at me. It was kind of cute.

"You good over there, Lo Lo?" Dre asked.

"Look at you, trying to act as if you're really concerned about my wellbeing," I said sarcastically. He chuckled a bit.

"Don't do me like that, baby girl. I really am. You know this wicked ass city we live in ain't right. Any one of us could've been laying up in the medical examiner's office tonight."

"You're right, Dre. You know I've grown up accustomed to how things go in this lifestyle. That's why I feel it's important for me to be my own woman and provide a decent life for myself. That shit back at the club scared the fuck out of me. I thought one of us was going to die."

Dre looked to be thinking deeply of everything I was saying. *He's sure been acting strange tonight.* We pulled up to my condo at The Harborview Towers.

"I appreciate the ride home, Deandre."

"Since when you start speaking the government names out loud, Logan." He chuckled.

"Nigga, ain't nobody around us." I laughed.

"Let me walk you in so that I know you're safe. Plus, I gotta use the bathroom."

Shit. I already let this nigga take me home. Now he's tryna come inside.

"Okay cool." I began walking ahead of him, and I knew he was looking at my ass. Of course I had to add a little extra switch in my stride. We got inside, and Dre stood around admiring my condo. This was his first time being inside. He had only come by riding with Brandon before, and I always met them outside or in the lobby.

"This is a nice place, Lo. You got real good taste," he said, sitting on the couch.

"Thanks. I thought you had to use the bathroom so much?"

"You're right. Which way is it?"

"Down the hall to the right." I side eyed him.

I took a deep breath again. I swore it was already 3 a.m., but before I would be able to go to bed, this nigga would have me having an asthma attack as many times as he would have to retrain me on how to breathe correctly. Shit. I wanted him to get the hell out. I was beginning to get on my own nerves.

He came back out in the living room while I was in the kitchen getting something to drink.

"Do you mind if I stay here? I don't feel like driving way back in the county to my house. It's late as shit, and downtown is pretty hot right now since we lit the club up. I can sleep on the couch if you don't mind."

I rolled my eyes in my head. Shit!

"I mean, I guess it's okay. I will go get you a blanket and a bigger pillow."

"Thanks. I will be out in the morning before one of your little boyfriends comes over."

"Shut up, Dre. You know I'm single. Holla if you need me. I'm gone to bed, fool."

"Goodnight, baby mama."

I gave him the finger and went in my room to close the door. I was finally able to feel relieved. I quickly undressed and got in the shower. By the time I got in my bed, I was so sleepy it felt like I fell asleep as soon as my head hit the pillow.

The next morning, it had to be around 7 o'clock, I kept hearing a phone ringing that woke me up, but it didn't sound like mine. *Got dammit, I forgot Dre's ass is in my living room.*

"Dre! You don't hear your phone ringing?"

I nudged his shoulder a bit. He slowly woke up, looking around and trying to figure out where he was.

"Your phone has been ringing off the hook for thirty minutes. It woke me up," I said with an attitude and went back in my room, closing the door. I could lightly overhear him speaking loudly to whoever it was. I went to grab my phone and saw that I had fifteen missed calls from Shay.

I quickly hopped back up and went in the living room while trying to call her back. Dre was throwing on his clothes quickly, not caring that I saw him with his bare chest and boxer briefs.

"Yo, Shay called me saying that the taskforce came and raided the house this morning and took Brandon in on the murder from the nigga last night! Fuck! This can't be happening right now. We ain't never slipped up this bad. I gotta go!"

He ran out the door. I stood there speechless. It was like my heart was pounding out of my chest. I tried to move, but my feet felt paralyzed. *Not my one and only big brother.*

Who was going to protect me now? How could my niece grow up without waking up to her father every morning? Shit, without my brother's money, what was Shay going to do? I wondered if her daddy had found out yet. I felt my insides coming up, so I quickly caught my balance and rushed to the bathroom. After about fifteen minutes of crying and sitting on the bathroom floor, I got myself up and got dressed in some UGG boots and a PINK sweatshirt and hoodie. I hopped in my car, trying to call Shay, but she didn't answer. I didn't want to call my parents, because if they didn't know, I didn't want to be the one to spill the beans.

I drove like a bat out of hell to Brandon and Shay's mansion. All I could think about was who could've snitched on my brother that quickly. It had to have been one of those eastside niggas. I was in so much shock that I think God drove my car to their house because when I pulled up, Dre was pulling on my door handle to get me out of the car. I had gone somewhere else mentally.

"Come on in the house, Lo Lo. I'm waiting on Dom to get here," I heard him say.

My niece ran up to me with tear-filled eyes, and this was the first time she was this speechless in her short-lived life. I saw Shay laid out on the couch, crying. I picked Kennedy up and took her upstairs in her room. We sat on her bed and cried. *God, what am I supposed to tell me niece? I'm so lost right now.*

"Auntie, the bad guys came and snatched my daddy away this morning! He was supposed to take me shopping today like he did every Sunday."

"I know, baby. I know!"

I held her tighter in my arms as she continued to cry on my chest. I then heard a deep voice downstairs yelling.

"What the fuck did y'all let happen..."

I knew it had to be no other than my damn daddy. I slowly pulled away from Kennedy and laid her down, so that she could take a nap. I dreadfully walked down the stairs. Everyone looked up at me. There sat my parents, Shay, Dre, and Dom. My mom walked up to me, giving me a hug.

"It's going to be alright, baby. Where is Kennedy?" my mom asked.

"I just laid her down for a nap."

"Come on, Lo, and sit down on the couch."

Shay was still sitting there in a daze. I needed this bitch to get herself together at least for my niece's sake. She still needed her mother regardless. During these types of times, the women in my family knew to mind their business and let the men handle things. I was having such a hard time getting my thoughts together. I was so used to my dad and Brandon having things under their control so much so, that I didn't know life without either one of them being around.

"Dom and Dre, let me holla at y'all outside."

Big Rell

I couldn't believe my wife and I had to wake up to hear that my one and only son got locked up on a murder charge on a Sunday morning. I had taught his dumb ass way better than this.

"What the fuck happened at that club last night? I taught y'all how to handle yourselves better than this in these types of situations. Y'all better find out who this informant is. I paid Paco, Quinn's uncle, who owns the club a visit before I got here this morning, and I found out that the club's security cameras had not been in service in over a week, which further lets me know it had to be somebody in that other crew that ratted at the hospital last night!" I said sternly to Dom and Dre.

"It's gotta be somebody with intel because how did the taskforce know where this mansion is?" Dom asked.

"You've gotta point, young blood." I stared in the sky, lighting my cigar.

"All I know, Pops, is that I'm finna wreak havoc on this city until I find this snitch, and I will personally bring him to you!" Dre stated with authority.

"I will be back in charge until further notice. We will be switching up routes and stash spots for the next week. No more business will be handled in any new territory over east. Dom, you are the level headed one. Stay on top of things with the lawyer."

Dom went back in the house to take a call with the lawyer for Brandon.

"You know I look at you like my second son."

"I know. You practically raised me."

"What's this I hear about you trying to pursue Logan?"

I looked him straight in the eyes.

"Well I, uh—"

"Listen… at this point, you will have my blessing with everything going on. Me, your mom, and Shontrice always knew you had a crush on baby girl since y'all were kids. But if you fuck up, not only will you have to answer to God, but you will answer to me, first!"

"Thanks, Pops. I promise to do big right by her."

We shook hands, and I went back in the house to get Shontrice so that we could leave. We were taking Kennedy with us until I felt her mother was stable enough. I wanted to protect my only grandchild by any means, and ain't no telling who her weak minded mother would have her around while my son was gone. I was officially back out of retirement. My son ruled with an iron fist. Mine was lethal.

Logan

I had finally gotten myself together out of whatever daze I was in when I noticed my parents getting Kennedy's belongings together. Shay reluctantly helped them, but she knew better than to go against my dad's word. Dom had left to go home and check on Malia and their kids. Dre came and sat down next to me as I sat on the couch with my arms folded across my chest, staring at the television but not really watching it.

"Aye, Lo. Let me take you to get something to eat or something."

"Nah, I'm fine. I just want to go home and chill. I don't feel like eating at the moment," I said dryly, not looking at him. I kind of felt bad for blowing him off like that, but I just wasn't feeling anybody at the moment. I jumped up, leaving Dre sitting there, got in my car quickly, and sped my way home. I made it home and laid on my couch, watching reruns of *Real Housewives of Atlanta*. After about an hour of kicking back, I heard a knock on my door. When I went to open it, it was my girls Kelsi and Quinn. They were standing there with Chinese food and wine coolers. I welcomed them in, fighting back tears. Nobody close to me had ever seen me sweat or cry before. I was always the strong one, but my brother was my heart.

"Got damn, Lo Lo. This is some awful shit! You think you're gonna make it in to work tomorrow night?" Kelsi asked.

"Girl, I already called out for the entire week."

"Lo, you will be just fine. Take as much time off as you need, but you are a damn trooper. You got this, bitch!" Quinn said dramatically. We sat around watching housewives. I was beginning to feel better. I loved my girls. They kept me grounded. My phone buzzed.

Unknown: Lola Bunny come downstairs and meet me in the lobby.

Me: Who is this?

Unknown: Come downstairs and you will see…

Who in the entire fuck could this be, let alone know where I live?

Me being curious, I slipped my UGGS boots back on and went in my room to grab my Glock-40 to slip under my sweatshirt.

"Y'all, I will be right back. I think I left my phone charger in my damn car," I lied.

I got down to the lobby of my building and didn't see anybody but the usual concierge staff. I looked around perplexed and then decided to walk outside, gripping my gun the closer I got to the door. I saw an all-black Mercedes G-Wagon parked out front. I didn't have a problem having to play tough girl every now and then. My daddy taught me well. Shit, whoever this fool was had the nerve to pull up where I lived, and my current state of mind would allow me to do anything in order to protect myself at this point. I stood for a second, and then Dre hopped out of the driver's side. A rush of relief fell over me. This nigga was crazy!

"Negro, what the hell is wrong with you?"

"What I do to you, baby mama?"

He smiled deviously.

"So you think just because I let you sleep on my couch one night that you can just pop up on me like this whenever you feel like it?"

"Calm down, baby girl," he said, raising his hands in the air. "I was just trying to check up on you since you left me in the dust earlier. Regardless, you still family, and I really care about you."

He grabbed both of my hands and looked deep into my eyes. I stood there in shock. My body temperature started rising rapidly. I was beginning to have the same feeling I had in the gas station the other day. It was a damn shame this nigga kept having this effect on me. My mouth wouldn't move. *Shit, Logan. You gotta say something!*

"Let me take you out tonight to dinner, Lo," he said, looking in my eyes for an answer."

"Okay, cool," I said with hesitation, letting my guard down for the first time.

"You upstairs by yourself?"

"No. My girls are keeping me company."

"Good. Better not be no niggas laying in MY bed!"

I laughed. "What is that supposed to mean, fool? I only agreed to dinner. That's it!"

"Yeah, that's what you think. Be ready at eight. I must finish handling this shit for B-Mac. See you later, baby mama."

He kissed my cheek and then walked back to his truck.

"Stop calling me that!" I yelled to his back. He looked back at me, licking his lips. That was one goofy ass nigga. I went to walk back toward the elevator, and I squealed like a little schoolgirl seeing her crush. It had been a while since a man had made me feel that way. When I got back in my condo, the girls were still lying back on the couch and watching the show.

"So who was the mystery man you just met with downstairs, bitch?" Quinn asked. Kelsi burst out laughing.

"What are y'all grilling me for? I went to get my damn charger," I said, rolling my eyes.

"Whatever, bitch. Your charger is laying right next to the microwave," Kelsi pointed out.

Shit!

"Ugh! It was Dre. Damn, y'all happy?" I said, sitting in between them on the couch. They both screamed.

"He's taking me out to dinner at eight." I grabbed my phone to save his phone number before I forgot which number was his.

"Oh my gosh, bitch. We gotta help you get ready! Get the hell up!" Quinn screamed dramatically.

"Were you really gonna keep that from us, whore?" Kelsi asked.

I just started laughing. *Hell yeah! I was!* Those bitches pushed me in the bathroom. I took care of my hygiene. When I stepped back in my room, these bitches had an entire outfit and shoes waiting for me. Quinn did my makeup, and Kelsi wand curled my hair. You would've thought I was going to prom the way these bitches were acting. I was only going to dinner with the nigga. Damn!

"Aww, Lo. You look beautiful!" Kelsi said.

"Yesssss, bitch. Yes. It's seven-thirty!" Quinn yelled.

"Thanks, girls. Can somebody go in the kitchen and fix me a very strong drink, preferably mixed with some type of tequila? My pussy is jumping. My nerves got me on a thousand right now."

"Got you, baby cakes." Kelsi said.

Dre: Baby mama

Me: Yeah Dre...

Dre: U ready yet?

Me: Waiting on you

Dre: Say no more...

Quinn grabbed my phone out my hands before I could even reply back, reading over our texts. "Damn, how you know that was even Dre I was texting?"

"Because I saw it all over your face!"

Kelsi came in, passing me my drink. "Well, Dre will be pulling up shortly, so what y'all bitches doing? Y'all spending the night or leaving?"

"We will be leaving in a few minutes. It's no need for us to be cock blocking. You might get some tonight," Kelsi said, and we all laughed.

"But seriously, I'm nervous as shit, y'all. All this shit that has transpired in the last couple of days is too much for me to handle, let alone if Brandon and Daddy find out me and Dre were out together like this. I'm good as dead!"

"Lo Lo, be quiet. I've been around your family since we were kids. Just relax, and nine times out of ten, if Dre had the nerve enough to ask you out, then both of them already know what's up. Dre wouldn't ask you to dinner without some kind of permission. He knows it's rules to this empire/street shit," Quinn stated.

"You're right. I have to chill. I didn't think about it that way. You make a good point, on that note."

"Alright, Quinn. Let's get up out of here. The little heiress needs some breathing room. She has a big night ahead of her." Kelsi giggled. We gave each other hugs, and they left. Not to long after, Dre called me saying he was downstairs. I walked down to the lobby. He was getting out of the car to open the passenger door for me. He was looking like a whole entire snack. *Got Damn! It's a shame how bad I'm lusting over this nigga. This never happened when I was with Trent. Lo, keep your shit together, bitch!*

CHAPTER 4

Dre

I had been running around all day, trying to keep the flow of business going. Big Rell was trying to switch certain rules that Brandon had in place all ready. Shit was crazy. That nigga ended up not having a bail; we couldn't even get him out if we tried. We all knew they were gonna throw the book at my nigga. Life was changing in a matter of days, but we had to keep this empire moving successfully. Of course I wasn't gonna come at my man's pops on some shit, especially not when I had come to him about his only daughter.

I pulled up to Logan's building, not knowing what to expect. A nigga could admit… I was a bit nervous. I knew Logan wasn't to be played with. At some point, I would have to come clean with Lo and leave Candi alone, but for now, I wanted to see which way this shit would go.

When I saw Logan standing in the lobby waiting for me, I ran up on the curb a little bit. *Shit! She looked good as a mafucka!* It kind of threw me off a bit. I wasn't really used to pursuing a woman I was really in love with. Lo touched a spot inside me I didn't even recognize.

I had to have her by any means and all cost. I got out the truck to open the door for her.

"Dre, did you just run on the curb?"

"Yeah a little. One of my phones started ringing, and I looked down, not paying attention," I lied.

"Yeah right. Anyway, where we going?"

"National Harbor, but you picking the restaurant when we get there."

"That's fine. We can go to McCormick and Schmick's."

"Cool. Put it in the GPS for me."

We rode in silence, listening to one of YFN Lucci's mixtapes. Two of my phones kept ringing. The iPhone Candi was blowing up, and the flip phone was one of my lil' niggas. I texted him back telling him to hit Dom if something was going on, but I was laying low for the night.

"Dre, you can answer your phones. I know you got business to handle. I'm familiar with this—"

"Chill, Lo. It's me and you tonight. It's just called respect," I said, cutting her off. *I really gotta figure out a way to be honest with Candi and definitely Logan.* She was my whole heart and didn't even know it yet.

"So what exactly is this 'it,' Dre?"

"What you mean?"

"Exactly what I said. Don't play with me, nigga."

She nudged me in the arm.

"Alright, look. I will be honest. I want you to be mine!"

I looked her deep in the eyes.

"Dre, are you serious? How long have you been feeling like this?"

"Look, it's been years since we've known each other, and I've been in love with you since then, honestly."

I grabbed her left hand, rubbing it softly. She sat there in silence.

"I'm not trying to make you feel uncomfortable or anything, but with the current situations that have come about, I have to be real about everything I'm feeling."

"Damn, Dre. I wish I would've known how you felt years ago. Our lives could've turned out to be totally different."

We rode the remainder of the ride in silence, listening to the music, but the entire ride I still held onto her hand.

* * *

We got inside the restaurant and were seated in a plush booth. I pulled Lo close to me and kissed her on the lips. She was drawn back at first but then let her guard down.

"Damn, Dre, is all I can keep saying. I can't help but to think what Brandon and Pops will think of all this."

"I've already taken care of all of that. They already know. You know I had to go by certain protocols before I could even step to you."

She sat there smiling for a bit, and the waitress came to take our orders.

"Hey. Can you give my wife here a shot of Patrón, I think she needs to relax, she's had a long day."

"Are you sure, Dre? That's so strong for right now in this moment."

"I told you to chill, Lola Bunny, I got this!"

We ate and talked about Brandon's situation, and how we would be able to move forward with one another.

Logan

This was so weird for me, but it was also a stress reliever. It felt good being able to sit next to him so close and being able to let my true feelings out about him to his face, let alone him doing the same to me. I still knew the type of guy I would be dealing with, but something within me allowed my feelings to fall in to place. I just prayed I didn't regret it in the long run. I would sure be having a convo with Daddy and Brandon, who the fuck did they think they were to be giving approval about what man could come and go out of my life.

"Dre, are you ready to go?" I asked, noticing him checking his phones.

"Yeah, let's go get on that Ferris wheel thing or something."

We left out of the restaurant hand in hand. I could honestly say this feeling I had was on cloud nine. Who would have ever thought it would be us two?

* * *

So within the past few weeks, Dre and I had gotten really close. We'd yet to go all the way and have sex, but our emotional and physical chemistry was so strong that I wasn't sure how much longer that would last. It had been weird with the both of us going around our family together. Both of our moms loved us together. Now Big Rell was still hesitant, but he was so into putting his focus on coming out of retirement, that it kind of passed by him.

I wouldn't let Dre tell me he loved me just yet. I was still a bit scarred from my last relationship with Trent. I didn't want to feel as if I was rushed into anything. I just didn't want to be with somebody that brought the crazy up out of me, but Dre was definitely putting the pressure on me.

Even though I worked at night, he still managed to insist we have our date nights at least two or three times a week. This nigga made sure my fat ass was well fed. I mean, he called to wake me up for breakfast every morning, even when I yelled I needed to sleep for work. He just ignored me and came to pick me up, which meant that during the day, for the most part, instead of him dropping me back off home to sleep, I ended up with him handling business.

I would cook us some dinner if we didn't go out, and he would stay with me until it was time for me to get ready for work around 10 p.m. Up until this point, I still had yet to step foot in this nigga's actual house. A few times, he had offered to pay my monthly bills, but I always turned him down. I asked him numerous times who he lived with, and he always said he lived by himself with the bare minimum, like some type of true man cave or some shit. I didn't have much of a good feeling about that, but I just let it go. I'd still been feeling low about coming to grips with the reality that Brandon wouldn't be coming home to us anytime soon, especially since he still hadn't been granted any type of bail. Even if he were to have one, it would have been too high for my family to pay off without putting the empire on the radar.

Kennedy went back with Shay after two weeks with my parents, so I still took on the responsibility of picking her up after school while Shay worked at her hair salon Brandon bought for her a few years ago. Kennedy was so used to me and Dre together that she got mad when me and Dre weren't together picking her up. One day, I went to pick her up while Dre did an out of town run, and that little heifer didn't speak to me the whole entire ride to my house. Brandon wouldn't let any of us come see him until after his arraignment and sentencing trials. He was so stubborn, but we all knew he was good. He was a tough nigga to crack, and my family had too much respect in the streets.

CHAPTER 5

*T*oday I decided to take this Saturday to relax and be within my own peace. I got up early and went to get my hair and nails done, thanks to Dre giving me a quick stack out of nowhere yesterday, while we were riding around the city. I had never been a using ass bitch, but there was nothing wrong with a little extra funding coming from someone that genuinely cared about you. On my way home, I had stopped at Starbucks to get my favorite double chocolate chip Frappuccino, and Dre called me.

"Lola Bunny, what's up, baby? I miss you."

"Aww, I miss you too. Where you at?"

"Coming back from Virginia, looking at this car, make some dinner. I will be there in about an hour, baby."

"Alright. See you later."

This nigga always comes in interrupting shit. Then, he be having the nerve to be short on the phone all the time, even with casual conversations. I just want to relax with my me time but oh well, I guess.

I got home and started making fried chicken, sweet potatoes, mac and cheese, cabbage, and cornbread from scratch. I loved to cook, and I didn't have a problem with making sure my loved ones were healthy. Everyone loved my cooking. One day, I would open my restaurant, hopefully within two years. That was my secret baby that I'd been working on and keeping from everyone around me. A job was a job, but I wanted to wake up every day and do what made me happy. Life was so short.

My phone started ringing. I thought it was Dre calling to say he was downstairs, but it was Quinn's name I saw.

"Hey, Quinn boo. What's up?"

"Lo Lo, I want you to go out with me tonight!" she whined.

"Aww, girl. I wish. I'm in here cooking up a storm for me and Dre."

"Now Lo Lo, I love you and Dre, but he can't have all of you. We never hang out anymore. You have to make time for me too, bitch! You know I don't like people like that."

I giggled. "I know, pooh. I'm going to set aside a day for just us this week coming up to hang out."

"Alright, bitch. I will hold you to it, and I'm picking the day too! I will call you tomorrow. You've pissed me off enough. Love you, bye," she said dramatically.

"Love you too, pooh pooh. Bye."

Damn, I do feel bad though. Dre has been taking over my life and much of my time. This is somewhat what I was afraid of too. Men can totally take over your life. I've been so independent for years that it kind of feels good to let somebody else come in and take over a bit, but it's damn near 10 p.m. now, and that nigga called me around six o'clock

saying make dinner. Shit, I hope he's okay. You never know with this
street shit.

I picked up my phone to call him, and it kept going to voicemail.
I started getting nervous, thinking the worst had happened, to the
point I had cut all the burners and the oven off and went to lie down.
I wanted to call Dom to see if he'd heard from him, but then I didn't
want anyone to think I was already at the point in searching for his ass.
We were just starting off.

After watching TV for about an hour, I had fallen asleep on the
couch and woke up in the wee hours of the morning. I put the food
away and went to get in my bed, praying nothing had happened.

The next morning, I woke up hearing somebody knocking at my
door, and then my cell phone was ringing at the same time. I shuffled
out of the bed to answer the door, and it was Dre. *Oh fuck no.*

"Why you looking at me like that, Lo Lo?"

"Nigga, what happened last night? I was worried sick about you."

"My bad, Lo. Time got away from me. Plus, I didn't think you
cared that much."

"What type of shit is that? You had me making dinner for you,
and you just pull a no show on me? Like damn! You could've text me
or something! You thought I didn't care? I've been glued to your hip for
two months now. What the fuck!"

"Damn. You don't have to cuss me out, Lo baby. I'm sorry I fucked
up. You know how a man like me gets when it comes to money."

"It's not even about that. It was just a big sign of disrespect in my eyes."

Dre was sitting on the couch, and I was standing in between his legs. He pulled me down to sit on the side of his lap. He kissed me deeper than ever before, tongue dancing and all. I had to pull away for a second to catch my breath because he had really thrown me off my rocker for a second. Then, I began to start having that feeling he always gave me, the butterflies in the pit of my stomach, and my body temperature started rising.

Out of nowhere, this nigga picked my big ass up, straddling me in the air, all the while still locking lips, and he started moving toward my bedroom. *Shit, here it goes!*

He pulled my socks and leggings off swiftly and began flicking his tongue profusely up and down my damn clit. I was in fucking heaven. I started screaming so loud that my voice began to go in and out. *Fuck my neighbors!* I guess he felt my body tense up, and he suddenly stopped before I could cum. He began taking off everything he had on, tripping over his own feet. We shared a slight giggle, and I took off my shirt and bra. When I looked back up, I saw what looked to be a damn Anaconda staring me back in my face. *Shit! All of that has to go inside of me?*

I went to reach for his dick, and he pushed my hand out the way.

"Nah, this is all about you right now," he said softly. He stuck his dick inside of me, and it was on from there. I was trying to get myself together. I hadn't had sex in months. *I know for a fact I will be sore as fuck after this.* He started off slow, I guess he could feel the resistance, but we all know niggas liked that shit at first. My damn pussy started getting so wet that I was stunned myself. *Trent never had me like this, and especially not on our first time.*

"Damn, Lo baby. You wet as fuck! This is only my pussy. You hear me?"

He flipped me over on my knees, hitting it from the back. I couldn't even get my words out. I tried shaking my head yes. Then he slapped me on my ass, still pounding me from behind.

"Mmmmmm, Dre! Oh my—"

"That's not what I asked. Who does this pussy belong to?"

All you could hear was my ass clapping in the air.

"You, Dre. You!" I was finally able to yell out.

"Don't ever give my shit up, Logan!"

He moved me on my back with my legs pinned on his chest but over my head. A few minutes later, both of our legs started shaking a bit. I guess neither one of us could take the pressure anymore. We came at the same time. That was a first for me. I never came with any of my sexual partners. Shit, half the time with Trent, I would go in the bathroom to finish the job.

He collapsed on me, and we began kissing again. *Yes! Sunday morning wood! It has been a while. Shit, I didn't even make him put on a damn condom!* Then he got up and stretched but held out his hand for me to go in the bathroom with him.

He turned on the shower. I stood there wondering what he had planned on doing next while admiring his nice firm ass from behind. He turned back around and began to lick my nipples with both of my D-cups in his hands and mouth. Then he pulled me into the shower as he sat down on the stone bench that was inside my shower, and he had me sit on top of him backward while he kissed my back, playing with my nipples.

I began riding his dick in the backward cowgirl position, and when I took a glance back, this nigga's face was so fucked up. He was in heaven. I had to turn away before I laughed. It just made me bounce up and down on his dick even harder. Dre came long and hard. We were both satisfied. I grabbed a washcloth and began rubbing him down and massaging his shoulders. We both were so relaxed and comfortable in the moment. It felt amazing. We finally got out of the shower, and he lotioned my whole body down for me. We laid in the bed, taking a nap.

Dre

Damn, I felt bad about what I'd done to Logan last night. I had every intention on going to her house to spend the evening with her for dinner, but Candi kept calling and saying if I didn't come home, she would call my probation officer on me. I had to come past first thing smoking this morning. I didn't want to fuck her mind up. I knew she would be worried, but I couldn't face telling her the truth at that moment. Shit was fucked up. I had to make some moves quick. Between me and Dom having to pick up the load of Brandon being gone and Candi fighting to stay relevant in my life, I felt like I was going to lose it any day now. One thing was for sure. I couldn't lose Logan, no matter what.

I laid there, staring at the ceiling while Lo was asleep after being dickmitized by me. She looked so beautiful and at peace. *Got damn her pussy is A fucking one. I ain't never giving that shit up. She don't even know that she is my wife from this day forward. Fuck it. This morning's events just put the cherry on top. It's a done deal.* My phone had started ringing. It was my mother, so I would call her back later.

Logan woke up.

"What time is it? Was that my phone ringing?" she asked in her sleepy voice.

"Nah, it was my mother calling me. It's about noon. Come on and wake up. Finish that dinner you started yesterday. A nigga is starving."

"You shouldn't be starving. You sure had a mouth full this morning," she said, pointing to her pussy.

"You got jokes."

I laughed. She got up off the bed. I smacked her ass and turned on the TV to ESPN while she went in the kitchen to warm up the food. *My thug ass really loves this woman.*

A few minutes later, Candi started blowing up my phone. Of course I ignored her annoying ass. On top of that, I think she'd been tricking outside of the club, and I definitely did not want any parts of that, but I needed her in order to keep a good address for my probation. Not too many places rented to convicted felons.

Dom: *Tomorrow meet me at warehouse east early.*

Me: *Ard*

I had told Dom's ass stop using these fucking phones to text out location spots, but if he was that serious about letting me know, he must've found out some shit.

"Dre! Come on!" Logan yelled. I walked in the kitchen, and my mouth instantly started watering. My baby could cook her ass off.

"Lo, you really need to quit that job, and let me open you a restaurant or catering business. Your food is the shit. Even when we were kids, I remember everyone loved your cooking," I said between bites.

"Aww. I know, Dre, but I wouldn't feel comfortable with you doing that or any man for that matter. I would rather save the money and do it on my own."

"See… that's your problem, I am not just any man. I am your man."

She blushed.

"My man?"

"Yeah. Remember earlier when I slid all up in that thing and asked you whose pussy did it belong to?"

"Yeah, but that is just sex talk, Dre. That's what all y'all niggas be saying," she said, biting her cornbread.

"I'm not any ol' nigga, so don't keep comparing me, Lo. Real shit, I wanna see you go places past this empire and everyday Baltimore shit. I love you, so I wanna help you in any way that I can."

I looked her deep in the eyes as we sat across from each other at the table.

"Damn, Dre. What am I supposed to say to that?"

"Nothing at all, baby. Your man got you."

I blew a kiss at her. We stayed in the house for the remainder of the day, watching movies and catching up on each other's lives. We talked about work, vacations, exes, you name it. Our chemistry was out of this world. Even though I already had asked permission to go after her, I keep battling in my mind whether I should really pull her into my wicked ass way of life?

When I was younger, I was always the bad boy or class clown in school. My mother worked so hard for me to do better and have a more stable mind, but just like many other young Black men, we fell victim to growing up without their fathers. I had a cold heart on the inside since the day I found out my father was killed, and there was no stopping me ever since then.

We ended up fucking a few more times throughout the evening. I was officially addicted to her pussy. I turned my phones off. I didn't want any other bitches I had to be hitting my phone. They would ruin my whole mood for the day. Sundays were our days off from the streets anyway, so my niggas already knew not to hit me up but for so much.

CHAPTER 6

Dre

I met Dom over east at the warehouse this morning around 6:00. He told me he had a surprise for me. I had crept out of the bed with Logan, not wanting to wake her. *I wore that ass out all day yesterday.* I pulled up to see not only his car, but Big Rell's car too. *What the hell?*

Big Rell never felt the need to get up this early. In his mind, he'd already paid his dues, so this shit had to have been important. I walked in the warehouse with my gun by my side just in case some shit was to pop off. I came around the dark corner and was surprised to see Dom and Big Rell had the other three east side niggas we had beef with from the club tied up in chairs. They looked to have already been beaten up pretty bad. Three of our lil' niggas were standing behind each one of them, so I figured they were the ones to do the damage. I was a bit mad that I had missed out on the prior action. We heard them lil' niggas planned on ratting out Brandon, and this empire wasn't having it. The streets talked, but these niggas were dumb enough to still be walking around like they weren't breaking the code.

"What you tryna do, Dre? I see you ready to let off a few rounds,"

Dom said, looking down at my strap in hand.

"He knows what to do," Big Rell said, puffing on his big ass cigar.

I passed each one of our guys a stack and told them to go ahead home. Wasting no time, I went down the line, shooting each one of them in the head without thinking twice. It seemed as if every time I had to kill somebody, I was getting revenge for my father's death in some kind of sick way. It was hard living with that shit, but I just dealt with it. It took a lot for certain people to become cold and heartless, but life was really cheap in Baltimore, and we all knew it.

"The clean-up crew should be here in about five minutes. I'm gone," Big Rell stated. He had a personal vendetta against them niggas because of everything that went down with Brandon. It was eating him alive to see B-Mac go out like that.

Dom and I waited for the clean-up crew to come before we left.

"How are things going with Logan, champ?"

"So far so good. I can't complain. I just gotta get rid of these bitches, Candi being the main one. The other ones, I can just ignore."

"You better hurry up, nigga. What the fuck you waiting for?"

"Man, I don't know. It's a lot of shit tied up between me and Candi, yo, but I never loved her."

"Damn, nigga… you and your secrets. I'ma just leave that shit alone. Don't get yourself killed over no shit you can control before it happens."

Damn, this nigga has a point. The crew came in, and we parted ways. I had to head back downtown to meet up with an owner of a yacht that I had looked up in order to put my deposit down to hold our spot before somebody else got it. I wanted a dinner date on the water with just me and Logan tonight. I needed to keep testing her to see exactly where her mind was before I would go any further. I stayed out all day so that I wouldn't have to go home and face Candi.

Logan

I woke up to not see or feel Dre next to me. I saw he had texted me, letting me know he had business to take care of early this morning, and he didn't want to wake me up. Honestly, the way he had dicked me down all day yesterday, I was sure I was calling the cows, and by me being on vacation this week, I was taking full advantage of being home and doing nothing. I got up to fix myself some breakfast. I ate breakfast while catching up on the latest season of *Orange is the New Black*.

Dre: *Dinner tonight at 9. Wear something sexy.*

Me: *Ok babe, can't wait!*

Dre was a horrible texter. That nigga had my feelings all over the place. One minute, I was second guessing myself about dating a man like him, and the next minute, I was falling madly in love with this hood ass nigga. I was just gonna let go and let things happen. I decided to get dressed and go visit my parents. My mom had picked Kennedy up for me today. She said she knew I needed some rest. I got to my parents' mansion, and Kennedy ran straight to me.

"Auntie!"

"Hey, princess. I've missed you!"

"I know. I missed you too. I haven't seen you since three days ago!" Kennedy said, holding up three fingers. I smiled.

"Where is your grandma and Pop Pop at?"

"Mi Mi is in the kitchen cooking lunch for me, and Pop Pop upstairs taking a nap. He said he got up real early this morning."

She dragged me toward the kitchen. My beautiful mom Shontrice would be turning fifty years old this year and didn't look a day over thirty. She kind of physically put you in the mind frame of Niecy Nash. She had on one of her long expensive La Perla house robes, looking like a true OG's wife.

"Hey, Mommy!"

"Hey, baby. How you feeling? Did you get any rest?" she asked while hugging me.

"Yes, Mommy. I'm fine," I said dryly.

"Well, somebody looks like they have a glow all of a sudden. What's up with that, shorty?"

My mom always tried to poke fun at the way me and Brandon talked but was trying to stay hip at the same time. Those young girls she had working for her at her boutique let her in on too much youthful information.

"Oh my gosh, Mommy. Stop!"

Kennedy laughed.

"Come on. Spit it out, Lo. I want to know more about what's going on with you and Deandre! Kennedy already told me he's with you almost every time you pick her up," she said as she made our plates.

"Dang, Ken." I nudged her playfully.

"Sorry, Auntie!"

"Well anyway, me and Dre are taking things slow. I understand he got everyone's permission before he stepped to me, so if you were worried whether or not he's holding up his end of the bargain, he is."

"You and that damn mouth, chile. Well me and Pam have been on the phone discussing grandkids and the wedding, so—"

"Grandkids! Wedding? Oh no, Mommy. It's way too soon for all of that. We may have known each other all of these years, but we still have to learn each other relationship wise. Come on, Ma."

"I know, but you know how me and your godmother can get a bit excited about things. Plus, she needs some company over there. Dre done bought her that big townhouse, and she's in there bored."

"That's what she has you for!"

I laughed. I guess we had bored Kennedy because she left and went in the great room to play with her dolls.

"I will leave you alone, baby. I am just happy for you."

She came around the kitchen island, giving me a hug again. "You know your father left out extra early again this morning. I know he's making his way back in the game on behalf of Brandon, but I am really not too sure about it. I made him retire for a reason. Look at the situation Brandon is in now. Your father is too old and greedy."

"Aww, Ma. You know Daddy is gonna do what he wants to do, but he is too old." I chuckled while she sat in silence, shaking her head.

"Mommy, you've always held everything together. How are you taking all of this in? I'm worried about you."

"Baby, all I ever did was rely on God. That's how I always prospered, and you can't forget that either, even in your own life. I can't say our family has chosen the best lifestyle, but no matter how much your dad was stubborn and in the streets, he took care of home and family first. He was a real man before anything."

I took in everything my mother was saying. Of course, I started thinking about me and Dre.

"But Logan, just because you made it to be a man in the game's wife, don't ever allow yourself to think that some of that street dirt and mentality won't walk its way into your relationship. Be smart and cut bad situations out as soon as they arise."

"No, Mommy. You know I don't play."

"I'm serious, Logan. I love Deandre like a second son, but I know what it is like to be a kingpin's wife. Situations will arise, and they have to be dealt with dead on. Now you're my child, and I taught you correctly. I know you know how to carry yourself, but just see him for who he is first, and let your intuition lead you."

"Thanks, Mommy." She kissed my forehead. I loved talking to my mom. She was the easiest person to talk to and never judged. I was so blessed to have a mom I could come to like that. I barely had to speak, and she just brought it right out of me, giving confirmation to everything that was on my brain.

"But look, I gotta get myself together to leave. Dre texted me saying to be ready for dinner and wear something nice."

"Aww, isn't that sweet! I have never heard of him acting like this toward a girl all these years." We both laughed.

"Tell me about it." I grabbed my coat, and Kennedy came running, grabbing my leg.

"Auntie, I want to go with you and Uncle Dre!"

"Not tonight, Ken Ken. No kiddies allowed."

Her eyes began to water, and my mom picked her up.

"Alright, Ken Ken. Haven't we talked about being a big girl, and you told me you wanted to make cupcakes tonight since you're spending the night," my mom stated, calming her down. I kissed them goodbye, I would have to holla at my dad another time.

CHAPTER 7

I was driving home, thinking about everything my mom was saying. If anybody knew how to deal with a man like Dre, she would. At the end of the day, I knew what kind of man I was dealing with, so of course I was going to keep my guard up when it came to him. For tonight, I was excited about whatever Dre had planned for us. I had called Quinn to tell her I was stopping by to borrow her flat irons. She didn't live far from my parents. I knocked on her door. Her little African sugar daddy opened the door, eyeing me like *who the fuck am I*. I couldn't stand his lazy eyed ass. He just always gave me a weird vibe since she'd been dating him the last six months.

"Hey, Fatu. Where is Quinn?"

"She's upstairs. Go ahead up," he said as if I already wasn't walking toward her room. When I reached her room, my face was still scrunched up from him eyeballing me.

"What's up, chicken head? Why you looking like that!" Quinn yelled with a blunt in her hand.

"Girl, you know I can't stand Fatu's weird ass. Why didn't you come to the door? You knew I was coming!"

Quinn laughed.

"Stop treating my zaddy like that. You know he pays my bills, so I just go along with the flow."

"Girl, where are those flat irons so that I can get the hell out of here?"

I instantly got an attitude. I cared about my best friend so much. I was the type to want more for everyone around me, more than half of them wanted for themselves. I grabbed the flat irons, gave her a hug, and then dipped. Usually, I would've stayed around having girl talk with her, especially to tell her about my latest with Dre, but I couldn't stomach things I didn't understand.

When I got home, I got in the shower to handle my hygiene. I was so pressed about making sure I picked out the right outfit that I was beginning to run out of time. I heard a knock at my door. *Shit!* I knew that had to be Dre. Thank God I had flat ironed my hair bone straight already. With only my robe on, I went to answer the door for him.

"Damn, Lo. I kept tryna call you. Bet' not be any other nigga up in here with you," Dre demanded, walking in the door.

"Dre, calm down. My bad. You must've called me when I was looking for an outfit in my big ass closet. Just be quiet and give me a kiss." I kissed him. He bent down to hold me around my waist and began tongue kissing me back. He softly pushed me toward the sofa while still hugging me. Then he pulled my robe open. He paused for a moment, admiring my curves. He grabbed on to one of my side rolls, making me feel insecure.

"I love this shit. Don't ever lose it," Dre said. Next thing you know, I felt the warmth of his tongue on my clit while grabbing onto my breast, massaging my nipples. This nigga was driving me crazy. His head game was out of this world. He continued to lick and suck on my damn pussy for about twenty minutes, until I couldn't take it anymore. I ended up busting all over his damn face. He jumped up, looking at his custom Audemars Piguet watch.

"Damn, Lo. We gotta hurry up. Our reservations are for ten. I'm glad you live downtown near the harbor."

I looked at him funny. I was still exhausted from busting a long and hard nut messing with him. I couldn't even say anything. I just found the energy to jump up and rushed to finish getting dressed. I heard him go in the bathroom to clean himself up. He still hadn't told me where we were going.

Dre

I couldn't lie. Logan had me whipped. I was mad as fuck when I tried calling her earlier, and she didn't answer. My first assumption went for the worst. The fact that I thought she was with another nigga, I knew I was tripping. My lady was never supposed to miss a call from me, so in my mind, she was cheating. Shit, I still lived with Candi but yet loved Logan, so I didn't trust anybody past myself. I didn't care how much of a good girl she was. She was mine. I came out of the bathroom, admiring how good Lo looked in that tight ass dress she had put on.

"Damn, Lola Bunny."

I crept up behind her.

"You look and smell so good."

She smiled. "Thanks, Dre Dre."

"Come on. Grab your purse. We gotta get out of here."

We got down to the car. I had copped a new all-white Maserati Levante.

"So is this why you went to Virginia the other day? To grab this?" Logan asked while standing around and admiring the truck.

"Sure is. And it's in your name too."

"What you mean in *my name?*"

She looked excited.

"It's all yours." I opened the driver's door for her to get in and walked around and got in the passenger side.

"Oh my God, Dre! But wait! No, it's too soon for all of this! How did you get a damn car in my name without me being there?"

"Lo, don't question me about that. You know what type of nigga I am. I love you, and you deserve it, so relax and drive us toward the docks at Harbor East."

"Thanks so much, Dre! This truck is the shit. I can't believe you!"

"Just consider it an early birthday gift."

About ten minutes later, we were pulling up to the valet close to the boat docks. Logan was acting so nervous to drive the damn truck. We had just made it there before the boat was pulling off.

"Oh my God, Dre. We are having dinner on a boat too?" she asked.

"Yep. Your birthday is next week, so why not start early."

I held her hand as we walked to meet the boat's owner, some rich white man. He led us to a table toward the back of the boat, and a waitress brought us a bottle of Moet Rosé, which I knew was Logan's favorite.

"Damn, Dre baby. I really appreciate all this. Shit… a new truck, a boat dinner, and my favorite champagne? We might as well get married tomorrow." She giggled.

"Well, why not? You already forever mine." She looked in my eyes.

"Deandre—"

"Look, Logan. I don't have much time to play around with my life. I can't say I live the best lifestyle, but I do take life serious. I'm serious about having a lady like you by my side."

"I just don't want to be hurt, Deandre." I noticed her eyes began to water.

"Me either, Logan. This being in love thing is a bit different for me. I'm sure you saw how my relationships were in the past." She shook her head yes and grinned. The little Asian waitress came over, placing our plates down in front of us.

"Hey, Miss. Can you get me and my wife another bottle of that Rosé? You want to come to our wedding next month?" She smiled and shook her head yes, not understanding me. I pulled out a few twenty-dollar bills and passed them to her.

"Stop, Dre!"

Logan laughed, tapping my hand.

"Where is the ring?" the waitress asked, pointing to Logan's finger. We all laughed.

"We are going ring shopping tomorrow."

I laughed. The waitress walked away.

"Dre, stop playing. She probably thinks we're crazy!"

She laughed.

"Logan, you know I don't care about what people think. I'm that nigga. Now back to our conversation. I want to ask you something." I got serious.

"Oh Lord. Go ahead."

"What if I got locked up and we had kids. Would you let another man raise them?"

"Dre, don't talk like that. It's hard enough for us all dealing with this Brandon situation!"

"Alright. I will let that question slide. But what if I went to jail and left you everything. Would you spend all my money and get rid of all my cars and shit?"

"What! Deandre, no! Stop talking like this. Are you forgetting I was raised around money? I don't need shit from you! I'm giving you a chance off the strength of my real feelings toward you! I'm not even the type to come in between you making money. Like if you got to stay out in the street all night until three and four in the morning making money, I would never blow up your phone to try and make you come home. At the end of the day, that same money would be coming back into our home to take care of our family, so why would I stop that. I know how shit goes in this lifestyle. I respect the hustle. I'm not blonde to none of this shit!"

"Look, Logan. I'm not trying to ruin the mood, but besides all this street shit, I gotta order my steps correctly and watch out for everybody around me, even the ones I love. I've seen hate and envy so much."

"Dre, if you don't trust me, don't lead me on, and just don't fuck with me."

I leaned across the table and gave her a kiss. I decided to just let it go. We chilled and laid back, enjoying the scenery on the water for the rest of the time we were on the boat. I noticed a few missed calls from Candi on my iPhone screen. I would just deal with her at another time. I had already placed her far out of my brain. We were living like roommates anyway. For some reason, she didn't get the picture.

Logan and I were stretched out on the front of the yacht as it was docking, enjoying the silence and summer breeze. Her phone started ringing in her purse, and I saw how she ignored it, trying not to be rude, but I told her to go ahead. She answered it.

"What?... Fuck no!... I will be there as soon as I can!"

I looked at her, trying to figure out what the hell was going on.

"That fucking stupid ass Fatu beat me friend up and poured gasoline on her until she was able to escape, locking herself in the bathroom. She said he came home from happy hour, drunk and acting crazy! I gotta get to her."

"What the fuck type shit is he on? Come on. Let me pay them their money, and I will take you up there. You ain't rolling up in there by yourself. Fuck is wrong with you?"

I paid the owner, and I flew up the highway with Lo telling me the directions to Quinn's crib. I planned on fucking this Ethiopian nigga up for messing up my romantic night. We pulled up to her townhouse and noticed the front door was wide open. I pulled out my gun. The fumes of gasoline had choked us up a bit. Walking inside, we looked down and saw the gas can thrown on the floor. We could hear what sounded like Fatu banging on a door, yelling for Quinn to come out. I eased up the stairs with Logan following me close behind.

As soon as we entered the room, I took my gun and hit him in the back of his head with the butt of my gun. He had some strength to him because he fell down and got back up faster than I expected.

"You wanna hit on females, nigga? Fight a real nigga first!"

I began pistol-whipping his ass.

"Quinn! Open up. It's me!" Logan yelled out in the middle of my rage. I guess she couldn't stomach seeing me like this. I was hitting him harder and harder.

Quinn finally opened the door, and she was unrecognizable. Her shirt and pants were ripped, and blood was dripping from her face. I had been a part of a lot of ruthless shit but seeing somebody look like that close to my family and friends fucked with me a bit, making me continue my rage. I was on the verge of killing this nigga, but I didn't give a fuck.

Quinn could barely speak. I could tell she was having a hard time breathing because of the way her face had swollen up. We both paused for a minute, looking at the damage I had done to Fatu. Quinn got enough strength to hawk spit on Fatu's body.

"We gotta get her to a hospital, Dre!"

"Nah, Logan. We can't. I will call the doctor to meet us at your house. Just help her downstairs to the car. I gotta call the cleanup crew."

Logan went down the stairs, and I shot him in the head twice with my silencer on just to be sure. It was crazy how quick shit could get real. I helped Logan get Quinn in the car. We drove to her house back toward downtown. I had known Quinn for a few years, from when we were teenagers, and we all used to hang at Brandon and Logan's house on the weekends. Quinn was doing her best to stay awake. I'd heard people with head injuries shouldn't fall asleep.

"Quinn, sis, what happened back there?" I asked her.

"That bitch ass nigga tried taking my life away. He came home drunk, wilding on me!" she said as she started crying. Logan was in the backseat with her, holding her in a bear hug.

I shook my head, rubbing my forehead like I always did when I was stressed.

"Did he have anything on you or any papers on him?"

"No. He was here illegally. The house was in somebody else's name from him stealing their identity like he did to a lot of people."

"Well shit. You good then," I stated, feeling satisfied. She chuckled.

"Shit, this will be my last, I've learned my lesson. I'm sure he was mad because he found out his brother tried coming on to me. Y'all know how aggressive and controlling some of them African men can get."

"You gotta leave them damn scammers alone, Quinn! I knew something was always up with him. His eyes never looked right," Logan stated. We made it back to Logan's place. The doctor was waiting on us in the lobby. Candi started blowing my phone up once again. Shit! I had to go. I wanted to stay with Logan, but Candi might call my damn probation officer if I didn't come home to her tonight. Quinn sat on the barstool in the kitchen as the doctor took care of her.

"Logan, come with me back downstairs real quick." I held out my hand for her to follow me. We walked to the courtyard next to her building and sat on the bench, side by side.

"Dre, I really appreciate everything you did for me tonight. I mean, I know the night was kind of ruined, but—"

I cut her off. "It's cool, Logan. I would do anything for you. I keep telling you how much you deserve it, but you know we can't talk about this shit with nobody. This stays between only us and Quinn. Logan, I need your trust and loyalty more than anything."

"I know, babe. We're in this together. I love you!" Damn she finally said it back. This would be the perfect time for me to tell her the truth.

"I love you, Logan. But look, I have to go. I have to get up early."

"Damn. I thought you would spend the night or stay a little longer. How much is the doctor bill going to be?"

"Don't worry about him. He's been on the payroll for years," I said, avoiding her first question. I stood up, pulling her into a long hug.

"I will take the truck tonight so that I can get it detailed in the morning too. Go ahead back upstairs and get some rest. I will call you to wake you up in the morning." She walked straight away from me. *Damn!*

CHAPTER 8

Logan

I went back upstairs to my condo, wondering what the hell had gotten into Deandre all of a sudden. I mean, I knew he had pretty much just committed a murder on behalf of me in a sense, but I always had been the type to pay attention to everything. He didn't think I noticed, but his phone kept going off, and every time he looked at it, he got angry. His eyes just now, when we were sitting on the bench, even looked different to me, like he was guilty of something. The doctor looked to be gathering up his belongings.

"Miss Logan, your friend is a trooper. I will be leaving two prescriptions for her to take around the clock. Please make sure she takes them. I don't want her face to become infected. I instructed her to take a bath and lie down. Do you have any questions for me?"

"No, thank you. I appreciate it."

"Goodnight," he said, leaving out the door.

"Quinn, you okay, babe?"

I heard her coming out of the bathroom.

"Yeah. Do I still have night clothes in the bottom drawer of your dresser?"

"Yep. I will get them for you."

"Thanks, Lo. I owe you and Deandre so much after tonight."

She began crying again.

"I was so scared! Lo, I thought today would be my last day ever, girl. I swear I am gonna stop dealing with the same type of guys and get me a real man in my life. That wasn't his first time putting his hands on me."

"Aww, Quinn. I wish you would've been said something. We could've just moved in together or something. You know I would not have judged you whatsoever."

"I know, Logan, but you know how I don't like asking friends and family for shit. It was easier just using Fatu. It was way too convenient."

"Well now you see how bad shit can really get. You want quality or convenience? All of this glitz and glam shit ain't worth your damn life, chile. Take your medicine, and get some rest, babe. You can have my bed tonight. I will sleep on the couch."

"Thanks, Lo. I really don't mean to invade."

"Only for you, babe. It's okay. Trust me. Goodnight."

Dre

Candi had texted me saying I had better be home by one o'clock. That bitch acted as if I wasn't a grown ass man. I was off probation in six months. That shit was taking six months too long. When I came in, Candi's ass was sitting on the couch grilling me.

"So what bitch had you out all night again?"

"Yo, Candi, for real… don't even bother me tonight!"

"Why not, Dre? I was out here riding around, wasting gas, looking for your ass! I didn't even make it to work!"

"Shit, I don't know why! I found out you've been tricking your way outside of the club anyway. That's probably the real reason you didn't go in."

"You got me fucked up, Dre! Day in and day out, I wait around for you constantly to come home so that we can spend some time with each other like we used to. At one time, we were the best of friends. Now you act like you cannot stand the sight of me."

"Honestly, I can't, Candi. You and I both know this was never a real relationship. It was just something both of us benefited from. When we first met, both of us were just trying to get back on our feet, and we used each other."

"Whoever this bitch is really got your nose wide the fuck open! I'm going to fucking bed. Fuck you, Dre!"

She rolled her eyes and went in the master room, slamming the door.

"Just be honest with yourself, Candi!" I yelled to her. I went in the guest room to go to bed in peace. Shit, I slept in there on the regular anyway. I got myself settled in the bed and began going into deep thought.

I had killed four people within the last few days like it was nothing. All the money and bitches in the world couldn't save a nigga's soul like mine. I was beginning to become so heartless that I was scaring my damn self. Now, I added even more stress on myself by adding Logan into an already fucked up equation. I bought her that truck, not only because she deserved it, but because I needed something I would be able to control her every move by, in my fucked up way of thinking.

Next, I needed to figure out a way for us to move in a place together, not only so I could get away from Candi, but also so I could keep up with Logan's every move. I was a man that thrived off of control, and I knew after tonight that I had her loyalty right in the palm of my hands. I loved her without a doubt, but a young hearted ten-year-old boy still lived deep down inside me.

My mother tried taking me to counseling after my father was killed but having to keep talking about his death only angered me even more. Then, my mother had gotten a new boyfriend that began beating my ass for over a year, at the age of thirteen. When I finally told her, she ended up shooting him right in the nuts in front of me one night, but I thanked God she was never caught. She tried taking me to counseling again after that, and the psychiatrist diagnosed me with a bipolar disorder. I refused the help when I saw how much it was costing her. I started running the streets real tough not to long after all of that. Big Rell tried doing his part by helping out, but the damage had already been done. I was already gone.

My phone beeped, breaking my thoughts.

Lola Bunny: *Thanks again babe, love you.*

Me: *Love you forever.*

CHAPTER 9

Logan

I was having the hardest time getting comfortable on my couch. I kept falling asleep and waking up until I finally just texted Dre that I loved him. I still had this gut feeling that he was hiding something, and it wasn't sitting right with me. It was about 6:00 a.m., so I just decided to get up to make Quinn and me some breakfast. When I was almost done, she must've smelled it in her sleep because she came walking out of my room slowly.

"Mmmm. It smells good, Lo Lo. What you doing up so early?" she asked groggily.

"I don't know, girl. I was just up with my mind racing."

"Girl, I feel like shit. My damn body is aching so bad, and I don't want to keep taking those strong ass Percocet and muscle relaxers the doctor gave me. You know I was addicted to those things two years ago."

"Yeah, I know, but if you're in pain, Quinn, you need to just go ahead and take them."

She sat down on the barstool as I made her plate.

"I can tell Deandre really cares about you."

"What makes you say that, Quinn?" I asked, eyeballing her.

"Shit, look at all he has done for you in this short amount of time. I wish his ass had a brother for me. Maybe I wouldn't have almost gotten killed last night," she said, teasing herself.

"Bitch! Just stop. I want you to eat, take your medicine, and go back to bed."

"Ugh! Okay! Let's go to the movies or something this afternoon. I can't sit in the house all day thinking about my fucked up life."

"I think that's a good idea, but we gotta put hella makeup on your face, and you have to wear some big sunglasses. That nigga Fatu got you good, baby." We both laughed.

* * *

Quinn and I decided to head to the movies this afternoon to go see *Girl's Trip*. I texted my mom, asking if she could pick Kennedy up from school the rest of the week. After that, I had put my phone on do not disturb because I didn't want it to ring while we were inside the theater. Quinn was high as hell the entire time because she had the bright idea to take all of the pain medicine before we got inside. Of course, this bitch ended up falling asleep and waking up at the end. I was so mad at her, but I got over it when she asked if I wanted to do some retail therapy in Towson Mall as her treat.

We were walking inside of Nordstrom's when I felt a person bump into me. I turned around immediately.

"Damn! Excuse you!" I yelled out to this ghetto ass looking bitch. She had all blonde box braids with her baby hairs edge controlled down to the max. It looked to me like whatever cheap ass edge control she was using had started flaking up pretty bad. She also had gold grills on the top and bottom row of her teeth. Then, she had the nerve to have on a tight ass white dress and Old Navy flip-flops with chipped toe nail polish. Her rainbow thong print was showing, and I noticed she had on a gold name necklace that read "Candi."

"No, excuse the fuck out of you."

"Bitch, it ain't nothing but space and opportunity in this mothafucka. If you want to square up, go right ahead and do it!"

"I don't' have time for this shit!" she said as I noticed the smell of Bud Ice on her breath.

"Oh no, baby. We both got time today. What's up?" Quinn butted in.

"Y'all young ass bitches are a waste of my fucking time. Fuck y'all!"

"No, baby. Your whole entire life existence is a fucking waste of time, especially with those dog ass feet!" I said, beginning to walk away with Quinn by my side.

Then the bitch had the nerve to pull on my fucking hair, trying to sneak in a punch. I didn't play when it came to ignorant ass people. I knew I didn't go out looking for drama. It always found me! I saw nothing but black. I went into a rage, and poor Quinn called herself helping me, but I hated for people to jump in my fights. I never needed help, but I knew I had to whip this bitch's ass before the fake ass mall cops could show up. For a thick chick, I moved swiftly. As soon as she pulled my hair, I swung back around and double punched that bitch dead in the face. She dropped so fast that it wasn't even funny. Quinn's high ass tried stomping her while I had her on the ground, punching her profusely in the face and body, but she damn near fell over, so I pushed her back. It was the middle of the day on a Tuesday, so the mall wasn't crowded at all.

"Lo! Get the fuck up. I can hear people on walkie's coming our way," Quinn said, pulling me off of her. Fuck! I hated entertaining people and giving them a reaction. I was far better than that. My parents would kill me if they saw me acting like this.

Quinn and I ran toward the closest exit we could find and did our best to run to the car. We could hear sirens in the background but thank God we made it to my car in the nick of time. I was so out of breath that my chest was getting tight, and as I sped off, I had to pull out my inhaler in order to take a few puffs. We were still on a high from the fight and didn't want to go back in the crib just yet.

I ended up going to my uncle's car wash in the hood down in South Baltimore. Even though Dre had bought me that truck, I still had to keep my everyday car clean, which was a blue BMW 6 Series Gran four-door Coupe. I worked so hard to get her without my dad's money. I would never give this car up.

We got ourselves together in the mirror inside the car. My weave was still all over my head. I didn't want to look crazy just in case my uncle was there.

"Do I look okay, Quinn?" I asked as we pulled up in the car wash line.

"Yeah, girl. You straight."

"Good. Come on. Let's get out. I will give one of the guys my keys so that they can run it through."

We got out the car.

"All that action earlier got me hungry. Let's walk across the street to get a chicken box or some of the Jamaican food."

"Yeah, come on." We walked across the street, and it felt like all eyes were lusting over us, even though we were pretty much dressed down, trying to be incognito today. For some reason, I felt like there was a particular set of eyes on me.

We got our food and sat in my uncle's office to eat. We both had him dying laughing about how I whooped that ghetto looking thot up earlier. He kept calling me "little Laila Ali." The funny thing was that even as a little girl, I always used to whoop bitches' asses. My parents wanted me to be a princess, but I was in school handing out ass whippings back to back, thanks to the help of Brandon teaching me how to fight. Bitches always wanted to be my friend and then talk about my weight behind my back like I wouldn't find out. I wasn't having it. That was how I got kicked out of five different private schools that my parents pushed me to go to. I ended up going to a public school like Western. I was blessed to have met Quinn there, despite it all.

We said our goodbyes to my uncle. By this time, it was around 7:30 p.m. I was on E from running around the city all day, and I could admit that I had a lead foot. I pulled up at the nearest BP station, and as soon as I opened the door to step my foot out of the car, I heard a car pull up behind me so fast that the brakes screeched when the person stopped.

"What the fuck!" Quinn yelled, looking in my rearview mirror. I got a closer look, and I noticed the Maserati truck.

"Oh shit! It's Dre. Damn, I haven't talked to him all day. I forgot!" I yelled out. Dre started walking toward me looking so furious. Even him looking mad as hell made him look sexy to me.

"Yeah, it's me. Where the fuck you been all day, Logan!" he yelled.

"I was with Qui—"

He cut me off.

"Don't come at me with all of that lying shit. I watched you the whole time you were at the car wash the last hour. Why the hell you got on these tight ass leggings anyway? I seen them niggas lusting over you when y'all walked across the street!"

"Babe, I'm sorry. Damn! I just wanted a car wash and something to eat!"

He ignored me, reaching past me inside the car and grabbing my phone.

"Put your finger on here to unlock it!"

I did it. He walked back to the truck and got inside so that he could look through my phone in peace. Shit, I didn't have anything to hide, so I started pumping my gas. When I was done, I just drove off toward my house. Fuck him and that phone. I guess this would be our first argument. I looked in the rearview mirror and noticed this fool had started following me toward the house. *Ain't that some shit.*

"Girl, is he following us?" Quinn asked.

"Yeah, that's his crazy ass." I shook my head.

"Wait. Does he still have your phone?"

"Mmm hmm."

I rolled my eyes.

"I don't feel like entertaining no bullshit for the rest of the day. I already fought somebody earlier. I just want to go home and take a long nap!"

I pulled up to the valet at my condo building. I didn't even feel like parking my own car. *Shit, I don't know if I am ready for this relationship shit if I got to go through shit like this. I am too much of a free spirit!*

I gave Quinn my keys and told her I would meet her upstairs. Then I gave the valet guy, Jorge`, my keys and went to get in on the passenger side of the truck with Dre. We sat there quiet for a minute.

"So what did you find?" I asked sarcastically.

"Don't ever lie to me, Logan."

It felt weird whenever he called me by my whole name. I didn't like this side of him at all.

"I didn't do shit, Deandre! Quinn and I went to the movies, then to the mall, and last the car wash! What is so wrong about that?"

"It's something wrong with it when you have yet to say anything about that blood on the side of those tight ass leggings you got on."

He pointed to my thigh. *Shit!* I paused for a moment.

"I got in a fight at the mall earlier. Some ghetto ass chick bumped into me, and we started arguing."

"You got in a fight for what? Logan, what were you thinking about? You are supposed to be my wife, and you out in public tussling with a bitch that probably wasn't even on your level!"

For some reason, I felt myself beginning to tear up. What the hell was going on with my emotions these days?

"Dre, look. I was only defending myself!"

"The next time, you either call me, or walk away from that bullshit! What if you would've gotten locked up? You are too classy for that type of shit. Here, yo. Take your phone. I will holla at you later."

He looked at me disgusted, and I felt so little on the inside. Dre had never dismissed like that. I didn't see what was so bad about me protecting myself. What he didn't realize by now was that my attitude was just as bad as his, so fuck it. I got out of the truck, taking my phone, and slamming the door. By the time the elevator reached my floor, this nigga was calling me.

"Hello?" I said, annoyed.

"So what? You don't love me anymore, Lo Lo?"

"Huh? What are you talking about?"

"You got out the truck slamming the door and didn't even say bye or nothing."

"Negro, you just laid my ass out! What did you expect?"

Quinn was laid out on the couch knocked out. I went directly in my room, closing the door and laid on the bed.

"I love you, Lola Bunny."

I hesitated.

"I love you too," I said dryly.

"I will leave you alone. I know you're mad at me. Call me later."

"Bye, Dre."

I hung up. He had just confused the entire fuck out of me.

CHAPTER 10

Dre

I had left Logan's crib and was on my way to finish collecting money around the city before I took it back to Big Rell. He had called me earlier, saying Brandon was going up for bail review in the morning for the second time. None of these lil' niggas bet not come up short tonight. I was already in a fucked up mood as it was. Candi had texted me talking about some thick bitch and her mixed looking friend had beaten her up in the mall. What the hell did she expect me to do? But come to think of it, Baltimore was big and small at the same time. I could guarantee that it was more than likely Logan and Quinn she was talking about. This secrecy shit was starting to hit close to home for me. I had to think of something quick.

I was so afraid of losing Logan that I was starting to have a hard time controlling my anger and trusting her because of the truth I was holding back from her. That was the main reason I went off on her. She didn't know of the stash spot we had across from her uncle's car wash spot. I was across the street watching her and Quinn the whole time while they were walking to the food spot when I heard all of the niggas outside tryna get at them. I was fuming on the inside. They were stepping into enemy territory, and they didn't even know. Then, it was one idiot that was bold enough to walk straight up to her while they were in the store. I was happy she shunned him off but still. I had two of my lil' niggas to push him inside the warehouse, and I killed him dead on the spot. There would never be a man that would be able to become a threat to any woman that belonged to me.

Me: *I will be late over tonight. I wanna hold you.*

Logan: *That's fine. You probably won't show up anyway.*

Me: *You still gotta an attitude huh?*

Logan: *Nope.*

Me: *Make some dinner. I want chicken alfredo…*

Her little stubborn ass was funny as shit. I wanted to slide up inside of her too. I guess that was our first argument. Shit, I argued with Candi every time I saw her, so that shit was nothing to me. But damn, I did love Logan, so I didn't want that cat and mouse kind of relationship for us. I was hitting my last stop when Candi texted me saying I had better come home tonight or else. I guess she was angry because she had gotten her ass beat today. My heart wanted to lead me back to Logan tonight, but as a grown ass man, tonight I couldn't even afford the risk of being with the woman I loved.

With Brandon away and me stepping in his place, I couldn't risk going back to jail right now. Shit, I was in my prime at the moment. I headed in the direction of my and Candi's house. I was so irritated that I took a risk and smoked a blunt the entire way home. I hadn't even gotten the windows tinted on this truck yet. I stopped at McDonalds to get myself something to eat for dinner. I had gotten so used to Logan, that I didn't even feel right eating Candi's cooking anymore. I noticed she started only working at the club Thursday through Sunday. I think she wanted to have more time in order to keep track of me.

Logan: Wyaaa....

I looked at my phone and shook my head, turning it off. When I got in the house, the smell of fried fish hit me, and Candi was sitting on the couch in lingerie, looking extra excited that I had actually shown up home and not too late.

"Hey, baby! Look, I made dinner." She walked up to me trying to kiss me. Her left eye was swollen. I flinched back a bit. It looked like it was turning black.

I nodded my head at her and brushed her off, heading directly toward the bathroom in the guest room so that I could get in the shower. Smoking two blunts to myself, I was high as shit. I hadn't smoked since the night of the shooting at the club. I sat down in the shower. I was stressed the fuck out. I was leaned back, deep in thought with my eyes closed, with my Boosie Pandora station blasting in the background. I felt a warm mouth wrap around the head of my dick. I thought I was dreaming. Whoever it was started sucking the skin off my dick damn near. My damn toes cramped up and some more shit. I felt the tip of my dick swelling up to the point of no return. She started sucking even harder, making those slurping noises.

"Fuck, Lo Lo! Shit, baby."

I couldn't hold back and bust my little troopers out.

"Who the fuck is Lo Lo!" Candi yelled.

"Candi! What the fuck you doing!" I yelled.

"Attempting to please my man, until he just yelled out another bitch's name! So that's who got your nose wide open!"

I jumped up, turning the shower off. I walked back in the room while wrapping a towel around my waist and sat on the bed.

"Man, Candi, get out of here with that shit! Why aren't you at work anyway?"

"Oh, so that's how you treat your ol' lady, huh?" she asked folding her arms across her chest.

"I will most definitely be calling your probation officer in the morning. I will be damned if you continue to cheat on me!"

"What the fuck you say?" I grilled her.

"You heard me!"

"Bitch, you are fucking stupid. If I go to jail, who will pay the bills around this bitch!"

I jumped up in a rage and pushed her, ramming her up against the wall. Tears formed in her eyes. I had begun choking the life out of her. She began coughing uncontrollably, and it snapped me out of my rage. When I finally let go, she dropped to the floor in a fetal position. *Fuck, yo. Now I gotta make this shit up to her.*

I picked her up and walked toward the master bedroom as she cried, kicking and screaming. I laid her on the bed, kissing her on the cheek, and then I pushed my dick right up in her. It felt weird as hell fucking Candi now, but I knew I had to make up for what I had done. Candi barely had any family that was active in her life. She was a foster child growing up. We connected on using one another and not focusing on falling in love, so I didn't understand why she had become so spiteful about my freedom. I flipped her over, hitting it from the back. I was there physically, but mentally, I had tapped out somewhere else. I had started thinking about Logan. Candi ended up cumming all over my dick, and I couldn't even bust. My dick was still hard just at the thought of Logan. Both of us stressed out in our own thoughts just ended up turning over and falling straight to sleep. *How was I going to continue to live like this?*

The next morning, I woke up to the smell of breakfast downstairs. I threw on some hooping shorts and a wife beater and headed downstairs.

"Dre, baby, I made you some breakfast."

Candi smiled.

"Thanks," I said dryly.

"Look, I am sorry about last night. I shouldn't have went off threatening you about jail time. I know you're on probation and backing up ten years as well. Let me make it up to you today. We can stay in all day, and I will just pamper you."

"Pamper me? Candi, you know I am not that type of nigga."

I chuckled. "Besides, you know I got runs to make," I said, grabbing a bite of toast and heading back upstairs to handle my hygiene and get dressed.

CHAPTER 11

Logan

*M*r. Deandre had me completely fucked up. That nigga showed his ass yesterday and then had the nerve ask me to cook and stood me up again last night. I think Quinn saw that I was a bit irritated and asked me to drop her off at her cousin's house after I cooked last night. I didn't tell her Dre was coming over. Thank God because she would've been asking me hella questions. He had called me four times this morning, but I ignored all of his calls. I decided to sign up for an online business school for business administration today. I needed to focus on my career goals and not some ain't shit nigga. I was going to spend my day in the house making my business plan.

Dre

I'd been trying to call Logan all morning, and she wasn't picking up. I knew she was pissed. Dom and I had to meet Big Rell at our main warehouse that was located way out in the boonies across the Bay Bridge a little past Annapolis, MD. Rell got a call from one of our Lieutenants that last night's big shipments of heroine turned out to be all fake product. When it rained, it fucking poured. All of these years we had the same Dominican plug, Emilio, down in Miami, and shit never got fucked up. He always supplied shipments on time and received his money on time.

Dom and I rode down together. When we pulled up, Big Rell was in a rage. I could hear him yelling on the phone before we even stepped out of the car.

"Dom! Dre! Go inside and look at that phony ass shit in there! This is some bullshit! I will kill Emilio my fucking self!" Big Rell yelled as he stood back on the phone, smoking his usual cigar.

When we walked in, the kilos were piled up looking just as they usually would, but then I walked closer, noticing the pack that Rell must've halfway opened. That shit was just as gray as the duct tape it was wrapped up in.

"Yo, this can't be real!" Dom yelled. I just stood there shaking my head. Death was in all of our eyes. I could see the money washing down the drain. I started going through the rest of the packages, opening them up, and they all looked the same on the inside. We were fucked. Over a $100,000 was gone!

"I just called, chartering a private jet for us to go straight to Miami this afternoon. Y'all tell everyone to take care of business as usual. I want Dom to head with me down to Miami. Dre, stay in the city. Get a hotel to oversee things and keep an eye out. We should be back within two days. I have a feeling it may be some other shiesty shit going on that had nothing to do with Emilio and his people!"

That was good with me. I didn't feel like making any extra trips at the moment. I think Rell had a point. I wouldn't be surprised if this had something to do with them niggas over east. Emilio never did us dirty, and we never disobeyed him. Shit, Pops had been fucking with him since the 90s. If we made money, he made money. Why would he fuck that up all of a sudden? I had to take Dom back home so that he could pack. On the thirty-minute ride back in Baltimore, I needed to let this relationship shit off my mind before I blew a fuse, especially after this morning's events.

"Yo, Dom. Besides all of this shit going on today, I already feel like I fucked up with Logan."

"Nigga, what the fuck you do now?

"I bluffed her out a few times, and I did some other crazy shit."

Dom chuckled. "Nigga, you don't ever tell the whole story about shit, but besides that, you need to be governing yourself a lot better. Shit could get real dealing with Logan. You knew from the beginning how her family looked after her."

"Man, I can't get rid of Candi."

"Candi? You talking about the stripper chick?" He looked real confused.

"Yeah. I ain't ever told y'all we lived together, because I never really gave a fuck about her. I just had to use her to come home from jail and get situated back then."

"Man, we are brothers before anything, and you never told any of us! I mean, shit… we ran the streets and gave each other personal space, but damn. We all thought you stayed with ya moms. I know for sure Brandon doesn't know this shit!"

He jumped up in the passenger seat a bit.

"Fuck no! My own mama don't even know!"

"You sure know how to hold a damn secret, nigga. Got damn! What's holding you back? Why can't you just leave and get a house with Logan?"

"Candi always threatens to call my probation officer, and the bitch knows I'm backing up time!"

"Nah, we can't take another hit like that right now. When me and Rell get back from Miami, we gotta get you up out of that situation, nigga. Next thing you know, you might start fucking up the money!"

He chuckled.

"Never that, G. You know that." I laughed.

I reached down and texted Logan.

Me: I love you, baby!

She didn't respond.

I dropped Dom off at his house and headed home to pack and to tell Candi I had to go out of town on business for a few days. Of course, I lied. I didn't want her to know I would still be in Baltimore handling business, or I wouldn't have any peace.

I ended up setting up a room at the Four Seasons Hotel in Harbor East downtown and rented a random ass Chevy Impala to get around in. The rest of my cars were too recognizable. We needed niggas to think we'd skipped town for a minute. I was gonna find out who robbed us and was out here selling our shit. I tried calling Logan again when I got settled in my room. She finally answered.

CHAPTER 12

Logan

"*L*ola Bunny! What's up, baby? I miss you!"

"Hey," she said dryly.

"Damn, that's all I get is a *hey?* I just bought you a new truck and everything."

"I haven't seen that truck since you stole my phone that day!"

"It's been parked at my house sinc..." he said lowly.

"And where exactly is your house, Dre? I've yet to come over."

"Look, stop worrying about small stuff. Just come meet up with me. I got some serious shit I need to tell you," he said in a low tone.

"Come meet you? You got me fucked up. I'm done with you at this point, and why do you sound like you're whispering?" I started going off on him.

"Lo Lo, meet me at the Four Seasons in an hour. You better be here before I bring you here." He hung up on me. The nerve of that bastard!

I shook my head and laughed a little. Shit, I might as well go to see what was so important. On top of that, I wanted to finish leaning on him face to face. I got dressed and put on one of my cute Fashion Nova activewear sets, along with my matching Nike Air Vapormax plus sneakers. I didn't want to be too dressed up and look too pressed. Yep… my pull up game was going to be strong tonight. I had to laugh at my damn self.

I pulled up to the valet, and I noticed Dre standing around the front on the phone. Once he saw me pulling up, I noticed he quickly ended the call. Everything he was doing was beginning to become sneaky to me, and that was a big turn off in my eyes! We'd been dealing with each other for a while now, and the heat was already starting to turn up. At the end of the day, I was responsible for my own happiness and positive experiences. If I didn't stand up for myself early enough when these red flags kept coming up, this situation-ship between me and him would become forever toxic.

The valet guy came to open my door, and with the swiftness, Dre was right there, trying to move him out the way to help me out. *What is up with this nigga?*

"I got this, my G," he said, taking my hand and pulling me out the car.

"Dre, that was rude. Apologize to that poor man!" I slapped him on the shoulder. I didn't care how tall Dre was and how short I was. No man ever put fear in me. Dre didn't say anything and just gave the man a twenty-dollar tip.

We walked in the lobby as I was doing my best to act nonchalant. I guess Dre could sense my resistance because once we got on the elevator, he pulled me into a big bear hug from behind and kissed all over my neck.

"Stopppp, Dre." I tried pushing him away.

"What's up with you, Lo? You acting like you don't love me anymore!"

I didn't say anything as the elevator stopped, and he led me toward the suite. When he opened the door, I was in awe. The Four Seasons always had the best penthouse suites. I began looking around, admiring the sheer drapes and custom furnishings. There were floor to ceiling windows on each side of the room, giving an amazing view of the inner harbor. I could be a geek for interior design. That was my silent passion, besides wanting to be a chef. I loved watching HGTV or any type of design show.

"Let's go out on the balcony, Lo." He looked like something was eating him alive. He remained silent as he opened the door, allowing me to walk through.

"Dre, what's wrong? I've never seen you act funny like this?"

He looked me dead in the eyes and took both my hands, intertwining them with his.

"Look, Logan. It's a lot going on. I know I can trust you. I got this room tonight because shit is beginning to hit the fan. We went to the big stash house this morning to gather the shipment, and it ended up being all fake heroin. Your dad wants for me to lay low in this hotel room while he and Dom are in Miami, until we figure out what the fuck happened. I have this gut feeling it wasn't our plug's fault but was something to do with the niggas we've been beefing with."

"Damn, I know Daddy is pissed. No wonder my mom called me earlier saying to keep an eye out for my surroundings. And then on top of that, Brandon isn't here."

"But it's something else I need to confess to you."

He looked down. I swear I saw a tear drop from his right eye, but let him tell it, something was in his eye.

"What, Dre? Spit it out!" He was taking too long.

"Look... I live with somebody." He looked like a sad puppy.

"Okay, so you have a roommate. What's wrong with that?"

"Nah, I live with a female that I'm not in love with."

I snatched my hands away from him, clenching my jaw up, and I slapped the dog shit out of him. *How could he do this to me?* He held the side of his cheek, and I looked at him, daring him to hit me the fuck back. My blood pressure was on a thousand.

I began yelling and pushing him.

"Are you fucking kidding me? Why the fuck would you waste my fucking time like this?"

He was speechless for a minute. Then with his long arms, he bear hugged me, pushing me up in the corner along the balcony.

"Listen, Logan! I only want to be with you! I'm just in a fucked up situation right now, and I can't leave!" he said through gritted teeth, still hemming me up against the wall like I was his archenemy.

"Fuck you, Dre! You know I deserve better! If I can't have all of you, I don't want any of you! What would my father think of this? He would kill you first then me second!" I tried slapping him again, but he ducked his head and let me go finally. I ran back in the suite, grabbing my purse off the couch, and Dre tried grabbing me again, afraid of me leaving. That pissed me off even more at the thought that he would think I wanted to stay there with his lying ass! I grabbed the computer desk chair and tried throwing it at him.

"Are you fucking kidding me, Logan? I swear, if I didn't give a fuck about you, I would kick your ass in this bitch right now!"

"And now you're threatening me, nigga! Kiss my big ass!"

I left, heading toward the elevator and fuming. He had me all the way fucked up! I got my car from the valet so fast. I made it back to my condo in five minutes. I felt like a fucking fool. I walked inside my house, still trying to play tough. Then, Deandre started blowing up my damn phone. I collapsed on the floor and broke down crying. I laid there for about five minutes until I got myself together in order to get up to take my clothes off and get in my bed.

If anything, I was mad at myself for letting my guard down so early on. His lying ass didn't even chase after me when I left him at the hotel. My mom always told me not to never let a man see you physically spazz out. That was when they knew they had truly gotten you to breakdown into their psyche, and anything after that, no matter how much love was between y'all, you are doing nothing but feeding his ego.

I looked on my nightstand to see what time it was. Then, I noticed Quinn's bottle of Percocet sitting there. I had heard stories from patients in the ER at my job saying that the pills would knock them completely out. I'd never been a pill taker, but tonight, I said fuck it. I wanted to go straight to sleep without thinking about anything. I didn't even care to look at how many milligrams they were. I was a RN, and I knew better. I took three, and it didn't take long for them to kick in. I was on cloud nine, and the feeling was euphoric at the moment. That was all I needed. I gathered the strength to put my phone on the charger and laid back, floating in my own misery. I was going back to work tomorrow anyway. I needed my rest.

CHAPTER 13

Dre

*M*an, this was some bullshit! I should've known that was going to go way too far left by finally deciding to tell Lo the truth. The sad part was that I think I was hurting more than I could ever really prove to her. For one thing, I was a nigga that always had a wall built up, and that was my first time in a while admitting the truth to someone I cared about. I had eyes on me, and I knew it.

Big Rell called me earlier to check in with me and told me to stay put unless it involved business. I couldn't even run after Logan like I wanted to at this point. I sparked a blunt and kept calling her phone back to back until my high took all the way over my body, and I fell asleep.

Logan

When I woke up that next morning, I felt like shit. I started brushing my teeth and immediately had to throw up. I had a hair appointment that I had to rush off to. Forgetting I took all of those damn pills last night, it took me a while to get myself together, but I made it. I had never had the best relationship with Shay to get my hair done at her salon. I still hadn't mustered up the strength to call my friends yet. I could only think of what Brandon would think. The fact he wouldn't call or let any of us visit him right now was bothering me.

I went into work that night and asked my supervisor if I could go on day shift for the next month or so until I could figure out my next move. I had to tell my mom she would have to continue picking up Kennedy from school for the time being. Deandre knew my schedule and was too accustomed to me being convenient and by his side. I was done with him. I knew Kelsi would be looking for me at work tomorrow night, so I decided to call her on my break since it was her night off.

"Kelz," I said with enthusiasm.

"Hey, boo! Girl, Dre has officially stolen my work bestie. What the hell! Got you putting in vacation time and everything!"

"Well, that is kind of the reason why I am calling you. I asked for a change of schedule so that I could be on day shift for a month or two."

"What, Why? Are you okay?"

"No, girl. It's such a long story, but some shit went down between me and Dre, and I just need a change."

"Do I need to knock that nigga out for you? Does Quinn know?"

"No, not yet. Tomorrow I want us three to meet up for dinner at Capital Grille before you have to go to work, if that is cool. They have to give me off tomorrow because I can't work twenty-four hours, of course, by me switching to day shift."

"Of course. It sounds like we have some serious catching up to do."

"Yes, boo, so meet me and Quinn there tomorrow at 7:00 p.m."

"Okay, love. See you then."

"Bye." We hung up. I walked out of the break room. On my way back into the emergency room area, I was scrolling on my phone and accidentally ran into one of the fine ass maintenance guys making him drop the cleaning supplies he was holding.

"I am so sorry. Forgive me."

I bent down to help him pick them up.

"No need to apologize, pretty lady." We stared at one another longer than expected until his walkie talkie radio went off, breaking our silence.

"Have a good night," I said, walking off.

"I will be seeing you around," he said, staring directly at my wide ass.

Damn, he looked all kinds of fine. He looked to be about six feet five and not skinny but not fat. He was just the right amount of muscular build that I liked. Brown skin and his temp fade matched his facial structure just right. I think I needed to begin dating a regular man like that. Hopefully, I would run into Mr. Fine again. Shit, I was done with Deandre, so why not.

I finished my shift up that morning, and I was dog-tired. I made myself a breakfast sandwich when I got in the house and went to sleep right after. Around noon, I kept hearing my phone ringing back to back. I looked, and it was Dre. I ignored him. I didn't understand him at all. I called my mom to check on her and Brandon's latest news.

"Hey, princess. How are you?"

My mom was always happy to hear from me.

"Hey, Mommy. I'm good. How are you hanging in there?"

"Chile, you know I'm fine. Just trying to figure out how to work this new iPhone your dad bought me. You know that damn Shay got a new boyfriend already. I'm scared to tell your brother!"

She started talking fast.

"What? A new boyfriend! Did she tell you?"

"No, Ken Ken told me yesterday when I went to pick her up. I knew that heifer wasn't any good. I should've let you beat her trifling ass years ago! I may go over there and whip her ass myself!" She went off.

"Mommy! Noooo." I laughed. "But no, that is terrible. Brandon is going to find out one way or another! She bet not have Ken around whoever the guy is!"

"But anyway, how have you and Dre been?"

Shit, I knew she would ask. "Oh, we're doing good and taking things slow," I lied.

"Mmm hmm. Well, your father is still in Miami until next week. I need you to come over and help me plan my birthday party after we go to Ken Ken's recital Friday."

"I will stop by tomorrow since I am on day shift."

"Okay, baby. I am not going to hold you. Love you."

"Love you more, Ma. Bye."

CHAPTER 14

Dre

I had been calling Logan for days, and she would keep ignoring me. I was going crazy. Candi surprisingly was giving me space after I told her about everything that went down with the shipment and why I was in the hotel all week. I had finally gotten a lead on what went down. I was able to find out from a junkie in Latrobe Projects that some new faces set up shop around there and were selling our dope with our signature trademark on it. Sure enough, I did even more investigating on my best private eye shit and saw it was exactly the same crew we'd been beefing with. I hit Dom and Rell up to let them know what was up and to stay in Miami in order to set up new routes with Emilio.

Today while I was out, I decided to take a risk and stop past Logan's crib. I wasn't feeling not being able to see her. I caught an Uber and went to the random garage where I parked the truck, so even if she didn't answer, I could at least leave the truck for her. After all, it was a gift straight from my heart.

I knew she worked at night and more than likely would be home sleep at this time in the afternoon. I knocked on the door hella times and kept calling her phone to no avail. I stood out there about twenty minutes until I finally gave up. I left the truck keys under the mat and gave the valet a tip to keep an eye on the truck until Logan realized it was there. I caught an Uber back to my hotel room. I didn't think it would be this hard. Most bitches blew up my phone when I fucked them and left them, but I had to keep reminding myself Logan was different. I texted Logan to let her know where to find the keys.

Me: I left the Maserati truck keys under your doormat. It's in the garage. Love you!

I sparked a blunt, sat down on the couch, and watched TV. My phone started ringing. It was my mother.

"Dre Dre! Hey, baby boy. How are you?" my mother said, excited.

"Hey, Ma. I'm good… just sitting back thinking."

"What's on your mind, baby?" my mother asked, concerned.

"Just trying to figure out how to get Logan back. I messed up, Ma."

"Damn, Dre Dre. Already?"

I sighed deeply.

"Yeah, Ma. And it's some crazy shit going on in the streets right now too."

"Yeah, I know. I was talking to Shontrice earlier, and she was filling me in. Well I can't help you with the street stuff, but baby, you have to do everything in your power in order to get your lady back. You know how I feel about Logan. Technically, she is my goddaughter, but as a man, whatever you have done, you hold the power to make things right. Now Shontrice also told me her and Logan are going to Kennedy's recital Friday. Maybe it would be a good idea if you showed up."

Bingo! "You're right, Ma. That's a good idea. Look, I gotta go," I said quickly.

"Now isn't that some shit. You're going to rush your mama off the phone after I gave you all of that good advice." She chuckled. "Bye, boy. Love you!"

"Love you, Ma. Bye."

I was beginning to get bored in the damn room every day, so this evening, I decided to go to the bar by the pool at the hotel. It was some nice scenery outside overlooking the water. I ordered a double shot of Patron and Cîroc Coco Loso drink. The waitress was a fine lil' short chick with one of those crazy short haircuts that chicks be wearing these days. She was petite with a little round ass. She wasn't the type I would usually go for, but the more shots I kept taking and the later it got, I began flirting with her. She told me her name was Ashley, and one thing led to another. I told her to visit me after her shift was over. I left her a large tip and gave her my room number. She told me she got off at 10 p.m., and I swear by 10:15, she was knocking on my room door.

I was way past fucked up. I sparked up a blunt, and we sat back chilling on the bed of my suite.

"I wanna taste ya dick," she randomly said.

"If you don't know what you're doing, then don't, but if you do, go ahead. My pleasure," I said arrogantly. I sat on the side of my bed as she unzipped my jeans and pulled my shit down. My big ass dick accidentally hit her upside the head before she could even start. It looked like the shit turned her on. She wrapped her mouth around my shit and started going in.

"Shit! Slow down a bit, girl..." I said, scrunching my face up. I sparked another blunt. She was sucking my dick good as shit. I was way in my zone. I ended up busting all over her face, and she didn't care. I had to kick this freak bitch out. After I came, she started looking too ugly in the face to me or something.

"You need me to request an Uber for you or something?"

"I thought I could at least spend the night here. I mean, I know we just met, but I thought we had some type of chemistry going on!" She looked disappointed.

"You can't be that naïve, baby girl! Here goes another fifty dollars. Find yourself a way home. I got your phone number. I will hit you up another time," I said, walking toward the door and opening it for her to leave.

"Fuck you!" she yelled. I slammed the door closed behind her, damn near hitting her back. It was around 2:00 a.m. by that time, and my guilty conscious was beginning to take over. Logan was back on my mind heavy, even though I felt like I didn't technically cheat since she was ignoring me. I still loved the shit out of that girl. I started calling her back to back.

Logan

I was sitting on top of my bed on my laptop doing my first homework assignment. This online class wasn't a joke. They had fast enrollment and got me started right away. My phone started ringing. I thought it might have been Quinn. I would just call her back in the morning. It started ringing again and again, breaking my damn concentration. It turned out to be nobody else but Deandre. *Maybe something happened with Brandon I should answer it.*

"Hello?" I said nervously.

"Lola Bunny!" Dre said, sounding weird.

"Yes, Dre. Is everything okay?"

"I love you, Lo Lo! You will always be fucking mine. You ain't going nowhere! I love you, girl. Stop fucking with me!" he yelled in the phone and then immediately hung up. It was weird as hell, and he sounded drunk as hell. Dre was more of a weed smoker than a drinker, so when he got drunk, he got fucked up. I didn't fuck with him anymore, but I was a bit concerned, so I decided to text him.

Me: U good?

He never responded back. After the call, I couldn't concentrate anymore. He was such a distraction for me, and I hated that. I called it a night and went to bed.

* * *

Today, I got off early and went over my parents' house. My dad and Dom were still out of town. When I pulled up, my mom was outside checking the mailbox. She was so beautiful. She had on a long blue form fitting maxi dress, and Shay had done her hair up in a high bun. Hopefully, when I reached fifty like her, I'd still have my youthful looks.

"Hey, Mommy. Don't you look like a beautiful, rich housewife?" I said, hugging her, and we went inside.

"You are so silly, girl. Shut up. What does Nene on *Housewives of Atlanta* say again?"

She paused, rolled her neck, and snapped her fingers.

"Because when you got the coins, they will make it in your size!" She twirled around in a circle. We both burst out laughing and gave each other a high five.

"Mommy, you have to chill."

I was still laughing.

"You know I love to laugh, baby. Did you find any locations for me for the party yet?"

"Yes, I wanted to surprise you! I was able to book the World Trade Center downtown on the twenty-first floor."

"Aww, yes. Logan, that is perfect!"

She hugged me.

"I will take it from there and call Tiffany the event designer, and I want you to cater it! You need to build up that resume, baby!"

"Oh my gosh, Mommy. I would love to! That would be good exposure, especially since Daddy will invite all of his high roller friends," I said, excited.

"Alright now. We got two months to go!" She looked at her watch. "Oh, come on, baby. We have to get to Ken Ken's recital. I don't want to be late."

I wanted to make sure my mom stayed in good spirits since her only son was taken away from her the way he was. I think I was going to have to do a pop-up visit on Brandon's ass. He was hurting all of us by trying to play so tough. He could at least want to see his daughter, but knowing him, he didn't want her to see him in that type of environment.

CHAPTER 15

Dre

I hadn't spoken to Logan since the other night when I made my drunk phone call. A real nigga started to bitch up over her. Even that little bitty Ashley giving me head didn't feel right. That was the real reason I had to kick her ass straight out. I had never felt a love like this. I had found out that one of the niggas from over east was a damn informant on one of my cousin's cases from a few years ago. That had me even more heated. I had gotten up early this morning and met up with two dirty cops that we had on our payroll. It felt crazy with me moving around the city by myself, so I was extra cautious. I told the cops the details of our predicament and gave them each $100,000 to kill the rest of the east side crew off tonight. They had given me a tip on where I could find everything that belonged to us. I ordered my crew to go collect our shit back from their stash houses and to kill whoever tried stopping them. I was seeing red, and the whole eastside was about to feel my rage.

I needed to hear from my brother, B-Mac. It had been too long. I was already a convicted felon, so us having communication was always going to be hard, and on top of that, Logan was trying to act like a fucking ghost, so that made my chances even slimmer at being able to talk to him.

I decided to go ahead to little Kennedy's recital. I went in the lobby of the hotel to get some flowers for the ladies. I asked the white lady working the stand to help me out. I was a real nigga. I didn't know shit about flowers. She had given me three big bouquets of all types of flowers I had never seen. I gave her a hundred-dollar bill and kept it moving. I made my way out to Glen Burnie, Maryland where the recreation center was located for her performance. I was really doing shit I never had done. It wasn't half bad.

I got inside and instantly saw Logan and Mama Tricey mixed in the crowd. Sitting a few rows up, by the looks of it, Shay was sitting next to a nigga I didn't recognize. I wondered if Brandon knew about this shit. I sat in the background of the center, looking like a straight up chump with all of these flowers in my lap, waiting for this shit to be over. Little Kennedy was the best dancer from what I could tell. Brandon would be pissed if he saw all of that makeup shit all over her face.

When it was finally over, the kids rushed off the stage to their perspective families, and I snuck up on Logan covering her eyes. When Kennedy noticed me, she blew my cover.

"Uncle Dre!" She held her arms out for me to pick her up. I picked her up, giving her a hug. I felt Logan grilling me out of the corner of my eye.

"Hey, Ken Ken! I missed you. One of these bouquets of flowers are for you." I placed her back on the ground, handing her one.

"Thank youuuu," she said.

"Hey, son! How have you been? Long time, no see," Mama Tricey said, giving me a hug, and I gave her a bouquet too.

"I know Logan never invites me over anymore," I said, staring directly in her eyes.

"You know how rude she is. Thank you for the flowers! They're beautiful," she said, pushing Logan closer to me. It seemed like her motherly instincts knew something was wrong between us.

"Can I give you a hug, Logan?" I said, still eyeballing her and passing her the flowers. She gave a fake smile and a fake hug. My heart damn near melted on the inside. Kennedy was standing on the side of us looking back and forth between us two, not understanding what the hell was going on.

"Oop! There goes, Shay," Mama Tricey said, breaking our silence.

"Hey, family," Shay said, waving at everyone. We all stood there staring at the clown ass nigga next to her.

"Who's your friend?" Logan finally broke her silence.

"This is my boyfriend, Turk," she said, challenging Logan back.

"Does my brother know about this?

"What's understood doesn't have to be explained. Plus, your brother is in jail," Shay said, grabbing Turk's hand locking it with hers.

Logan bucked at Shay, lifting her arm, about to punch Shay square in the face, and I wasn't going to stop her either. That trick deserved to be knocked out, fucking around on my brother all out in the open.

Jail or not, Brandon did big right by Shay, but Mama Tricey held her back. I stepped in and pulled Logan toward the front lobby. I don't know what kind of connection or chemistry we had, but I could feel the steam coming out of her body. It wasn't the time or place to be out here making a scene. Plus, Kennedy was watching.

"Shay, I will be having a very long talk with you in private tomorrow! Kennedy, go get your belongings from backstage. You are coming with me!" Mama Tricey yelled.

Logan

Dre pulled me into the lobby. *I feel like shit for losing my temper in front of my niece. I think it was a combination of being angry that Deandre popped up and seeing that disloyal bitch Shay disrespect my brother without a care in the world. Oh, baby, was I heated!* The steam was filtering through my pores something serious. I felt my hands shaking as I stood around, biting on my bottom lip.

"Logan... Hello there? You good?" Dre tried getting my attention. I had finally snapped out of it.

"I'm good, Dre. That was some bullshit back there, and you know it. Why are you even here?"

I got smart with him.

"Whoa, Logan. Chill!" he yelled. Mama Tricey walked up.

"Logan, ride home with Dre. I need to borrow your car," my mom said, walking up behind him with Kennedy on her heels.

"Dang, Mommy. Why?"

"Because I said so! I will give your precious car back, and besides, I think you and Dre have a lot y'all need to talk about! Don't ask me anymore damn questions, lil' girl."

When my mom got into one of her snappy moods, I learned over the years to just let her be. I reluctantly got in the car with Dre. I sat in silence with my arms folded and staring out the window. I pulled my shades down to block Dre from stealing glances at me as he drove up 695. My mother wasn't slick at all. She knew what she was doing!

"You can take me straight home."

I finally broke the awkward silence.

"I would've thought you wanted to spend the rest of the evening with your man."

I chuckled.

"My man? The last I checked, you belong to someone else!"

I got smart with him.

"I found us a house."

"Wow. So, am I just supposed to go running back in your fucking arms now, Dre?" I asked, pulling my shades off my face.

"You don't appreciate shit, Logan! All that shit I did for you in this short amount of time! I don't do shit for these bitches out here that I fuck with!" he began to yell.

"Are you fucking kidding me!" I asked, yelling at the top of my lungs. It was fucked up when the man you had fallen in love with was revealing how sick his mind was as the days progressed. I was a child of God before anything. I was not a homewrecker! I hated the fact that even though he lied to me from the very beginning, I still harbored feelings for his ignorant ass.

"Logan, just shut the fuck up, yo!"

"Who the fuck are you talking to? If I didn't fear for my life, I would try my hardest to fuck you up in this car right now!" I yelled.

Then, I realized he passed my exit going north toward interstate 83.

"And where the fuck are you taking me!" I yelled again.

He ignored me and kept driving. My head had begun to hurt at this point. I reached in my purse and took four of Quinn's Percocets. Lately, I had been carrying them around with me wherever I went. I didn't want to be present in this moment. *I am supposed to be doing schoolwork and revising my business plan, but now I'm jammed back up with this fool.* Dre noticed me taking the pills.

"Since when have you started taking medicine, Logan? What kind of pills are they?" he called himself quizzing me.

"Ever since you came in my life and fucked it up... and it's just aspirin," I lied. He shook his head and started driving faster. I pulled my shades back over my eyes so that I could zone out and be high. About thirty minutes later, I noticed a sign that said, "Welcome to Pennsylvania." We pulled up to a big mansion in some part of Pennsylvania I had never heard of.

"Come on, Logan. Get out," he said, coming to open the passenger door for me.

"Where do you have me at, and whose house is this?"

We walked toward the beautiful home.

"It's ours! This is where we will get married and raise our ten kids," he said, smiling from ear to ear.

"Kids? Marriage?" I asked, confused.

"Yep!"

This nigga is making plans for our future life and isn't even trying to address our problems that we're going through now in his face. He didn't even tell me whose name the house was in. We continued walking around the beautiful home. There was a huge double grand staircase with a beautiful chef style kitchen that I could only dream of having. I felt myself imagining how I could decorate it, but I had to stop myself and stop running off of this falsehood that this fool wanted me to live under.

"Do you like it?"

We started walking toward the front door.

"I love it, but we have to be real. What's your relationship status with the woman you live with, and how could we possibly move to be up here to Pennsylvania with both of us having to commute back and forth to Baltimore?"

"Don't worry about all of that. I got it all covered. You're gonna have to quit that job though."

"What do you mean? So I can stay at home with ten kids while you're down in the city running the streets and in and out of bitches' pussies?"

"Come on. Let's head back. It's getting late."

He laughed and ignored me. He actually had a nerve to laugh. I was being fucking serious! I didn't have time for this weak as shit. He could move his stay at home bitch in there for all I cared. I had to tell Quinn and Kelsi this crazy shit. This sorry ass nigga bought me flowers and showed me a random house, thinking it would solve everything. Never once had he even apologized.

We got back in the car. By this time, I was over the moon high after building up so much tension within the last couple of hours. Him having to keep slamming on brakes from weaving in between cars was the only thing that was keeping me halfway awake. Thank God for these shades because if he noticed me nodding out, he would have whooped my ass in this car.

When we got back in the city, his phone started going off. I looked down, noticing it was my dad calling him. It must've been important because he finally told me he was taking me home. There was a car in front of us holding up traffic with his hazard lights on when we were coming off the exit ramp, so he had to end up swerving around them so we wouldn't have ended up in an accident. This caused all three of his phones to magically fall on top of my lap. When I went to grab them for him, he went crazy on me. By the time we got to the red light, he'd pulled my left middle finger all the way back, causing my first reaction of slapping the shit out of him, sobering me up real quick.

"What the hell is wrong with you? I was just trying to give you your millions of phones back since they slid onto my lap!"

He sat there holding the side of his face, pulling into the gas station so that he could get himself together.

"I thought you were trying to look inside my phones," he said, still holding his left cheek.

"No! You must have something to hide any time you overreact like that! Ugh, just take me home for the thousandth time," I said, blown. I had a text message coming in. My phone buzzed. It was Derrick (Mr. Fine) from my job asking me how my day was going. I had gotten his number the day after we bumped into one another. I started smiling, and Dre was grilling me hard.

"Who is that?" he asked. I sucked my teeth.

"It's Quinn. Stop being nosy!" I lied. We finally got to my condo building, and I rushed out of Dre's Benz without even saying a word to him. I was beginning to feel like the more I poured out, his bad spirit was sucking me back in, and I knew better. I was walking toward the elevator, still in my phone. I knew Dre was pissed, but he pulled off just as quickly as I got out, so fuck it.

Derrick: Can I treat you to dinner and drinks tonight?

Me: Sure I would like that!

Derrick: I know it's too early for me to know where you live and everything so let's meet up in Fells Point somewhere... How does Ouzo Bay sound?

Me: Ok cool I will meet you in front of Ouzo Bay around 11.

Derrick: Sounds good to me.

CHAPTER 16

Dre

$\mathcal{L}$ogan's ass had me fucked up! I knew I may have been avoiding her and dancing around her feelings, but a part of me didn't give a fuck. She was mine. Not saying she was my property, but technically, she was because I had deep feelings for her, and I always got what I wanted by any means at any cost. In my opinion, there wasn't a need for me to be open enough to address her feelings. I was the man. I was going to do what I felt I needed to do in my own way. She would just have to deal with it. She wasn't going anywhere!

Big Rell had called me, saying him and Dom would be coming back home in the morning. Everything was set in stone. The two dirty cops I had hired had given me the "mission-accomplished" text just in time, and Big Rell would be sending them a big tip within the week coming up. Now the only problem was we had to form a new east side crew, and that would take time to feel niggas out enough to make sure they were trustworthy. If they were really into getting money, they would fall in line. I was thinking about asking Big Rell if it was cool if I brought on my cousin, Wesley, to run over the east. I didn't want to move anybody from any other spots. It might fuck things up in the long run. Things were running smoothly, besides everything else going on. I texted Candi to let her know I would be back home tomorrow in order to ease her mind.

Logan didn't know I got my younger cousin Sade` to teach me how to hack into iCloud accounts on iPhones a few days ago. I needed to know what was going on with my girl and what her moves were. I had to figure out who she was texting and smiling at. On my way over to the west to check on my spots, I was going through her latest text messages and saw she was texting some nigga and planned on meeting him downtown tonight on some type of date shit. I was on fire. I had something for her ass!

I pulled up at the corner on North and Fulton Ave and got out, going into the corner store to get something to drink and buy some cigarillos. I saw a familiar face at the register, and it was Ashley, the chick I was with the other night at the hotel. I walked up on her.

"What's up, lil' mama?"

She started smiling from ear to ear.

"Hey, D. What are you doing around here?"

"Shit, on my way back to the hotel."

I didn't want to tell her my business. I could've been anybody for all she knew.

"I live around the corner. I'm bored. Can I go with you to the room?"

I thought about it for a minute.

"Yeah, let's go."

I took her past her house to get a change of clothes and to grab some heels. We rode back down to the hotel, and I kept re-reading the messages between Logan and whoever that clown nigga was while I was driving. I saw that she would be meeting that clown around eleven, so I had a little time to smoke and get my dick wet by Ashley's naïve ass in the meantime. Why not have fun on my last night in my big ass presidential suite.

As soon as we got in the room, I pulled out a condom, bent Ashley right over the couch, and fucked her from the back, long and hard. She was screaming as I started pulling her hair and had my left leg hiked up on a chair next to the couch. Her pussy didn't seem bad, but it would do for now. Nothing compared to Logan's shit. I busted my nut, and she went to get in the shower. I didn't want to give her my best sex game, because it really wasn't a need to. I had already seen what she was about. I had rolled up and sat on the couch smoking when she got out the shower wrapped in a towel.

"So where are we going tonight?"

"That spot not far from here called Ouzo Bay," I said, passing her the blunt.

"I love you," she said, making me choke hard as hell.

"What you mean *you love me*? You barely know me," I said in between coughs.

"You seem cool to chill with."

"Shorty, just because a nigga seems cool doesn't mean you love him. You got a lot to learn, baby girl. Shit, I'm twenty-seven, and you're twenty-one. You got a ways to go and a lot more to learn."

This bitch was dumb as shit. She fucked me up with that one. I got up to get in the shower, leaving her sitting there in her thoughts and smoking.

Logan

I was extra excited to be going on a date with a new face. That shit with Dre earlier really had my mind on some other shit. I couldn't let him disrespect me like this. I was doing my best to stop giving these men chances to come in my life that were not valuing and respecting the opportunity. At the end of the day, I knew I was raised right with a good spirit and old soul. I knew my worth, and I knew what I deserved.

I put on a cute multi-colored sequined blazer and a solid black tube dress, with my black Christian Louboutin Daffodile pumps. I always believed in being sleek and chic but not over doing it on first dates. I met Derrick outside. He was on time, waiting for me on the sidewalk across the street from the restaurant. I walked up, giving him a hug.

"Hey, Derrick," I said, smiling.

"Logan, it's a pleasure to see you," he said, grabbing my right hand and kissing it.

"I've already reserved a table by the bar for us."

"Oh, look at you trying to be on point for the night!"

We both laughed going inside. We were sitting around, eating, and drinking when I glanced toward the door and noticed Deandre and some bitch walking in. To say the least, my heart was crushed. *Was this shit just a coincidence, or did he know I was going to be here?*

I excused myself from the table and rushed into the bathroom, trying to hold myself together. I looked through my purse for my pills. I needed to call Quinn to ask her to fake still feeling bad so that she could get another prescription. I took five pills, trying to wash away whatever feeling was coming over me.

Walking back toward the table, I noticed Dre and his little bitch were sitting at the bar next to our table. *Isn't that some shit!* I wanted to scream, but I held it together. I did my best to sit down without giving him eye contact. The girl he was with looked to be a bit younger than me. I got my posture together and started talking to Derrick again.

"I'm sorry. I had to freshen up and go to the ladies' room."

"You're fine, sweetheart. Are you enjoying this place?" Derrick said.

"It's beau—"

"Excuse me. Hey, Logan," Deandre cut in. My blood began to boil.

"Hello, Deandre."

"I wanna introduce you to my lady, Ashley. Ashley, this is Logan. Logan, this is Ashley."

Me and Derrick just stared at his act. Of course, Derrick was oblivious to what was actually going on.

"My bad, partner."

Dre put his hand out to Derrick, shaking his hand.

"I didn't get your name. Logan, introduce me to your friend," he said, staring back at me. I still didn't say anything. The pills I took had kicked in just in time. I felt like I was beginning to float away in LaLa land. The waiter came over, interrupting just in time and giving us our bill. He and little Miss Ashley moved back to the bar. *Deandre really had the fucking nerve. But damn, he looked good as fuck.*

Derrick gave the waiter the cash for our bill, and we got up to walk outside. We were standing outside waiting for our respective valets while having small talk about work. Next thing you know, Deandre came out behind us.

"Aye, Logan. Can I talk to you for a minute?"

Derrick looked like he wanted to bitch up a bit. He didn't compare with Dre at all. If it were vice versa, Dre would've never let me hold a conversation with a man in his presence. Derrick's car pulled up before mine did. I told him goodbye, letting him know I was okay, and he left.

Here we go! I wasn't going to be able to hold back my anger for too much longer, and Deandre knew it!

Turning back to him, I asked, "How can I help you?"

"Who the fuck is that nigga you were with?"

He pulled on my arm hard, walking me around the side of the building. Even though I was high from the pills, his eyes looked strange to me, like a killer was inside of him.

"He's nobody that concerns you!"

I pulled out my phone, scrolling through it.

"Stop fucking playing with me, Logan!"

He was getting even angrier at my nonchalant attitude. He pulled my phone out of my hand, throwing it to the ground and shattering it into pieces.

"You are fucking crazy! Leave me the hell alone!" I yelled out I was so mad. My phone was my lifeline. I noticed my car being pulled up. I went to walk away quickly, and Deandre pushed me to the ground hard as shit. I fell hard, catching myself from hitting my face on the concrete. I blacked out. I got back up in a rage, going crazy toward him, taking off my shoes and bashing him in the head with my stiletto heel. His face and head started bleeding. He paused when he noticed the blood dripping from his head and punched me square in my beautiful high cheekbone. I heard a girl's voice yelling for someone to call the police, which sobered me up. Then, an older white guy came around the corner, breaking us up and doing the best he could to hold Dre back. I hurriedly got myself together and ran away toward my car. I stole a punch toward that Ashley girl, knocking her down to the ground before jumping in my damn car and speeding off toward my house.

I had never been so upset in my damn life. I was too mad to cry. I wanted to throw up. The pills I had taken and the anger I had built up had my head spinning. I had to pull over on a side street near my house in order to throw up. I leaned over out of my driver's side door and puked my brains out. I couldn't hold back the tears anymore. I closed the door and burst out crying. I was able to get enough strength to drive up the street to my condo and decided against going to the valet. I parked my car in the garage myself so that nobody could see me in this condition. I parked in the assigned space next to the Maserati truck Dre had bought me. I got out of the car, kicking the side of the truck with my barefoot. I knew I looked like a mad woman.

I got to my apartment, stripping out of my clothes. My five-hundred-dollar blazer I had ordered online was in shambles. I looked myself in the mirror and got the shock of my life, looking at my bruised and puffed up cheekbones. I just busted out crying. It seemed like it was the way of life for me within the last month or so. I couldn't believe it. I needed my brother back so bad. He and my mom were really the glue to my life. Shit was fucked up beyond measures.

I turned the bathtub water on and sat on the ledge of the tub until I was able to gather myself up in order to wash my blood and Deandre's blood from his head off of me. I most definitely wasn't going to make it to work tomorrow.

I sat in the tub, wallowing in my own misery and pain. *That nigga really broke my phone. I have to get a new one tomorrow. Everyone will be trying to contact me.* I sat in there, still crying, and eventually got out, crying myself to sleep.

CHAPTER 17

Dre

I was so blown at how things had transpired so quickly. I never wanted to do any type of harm to Logan. I felt like a damn animal. *I fucked up big time. Fuck, yo!* I was able to push the white guy off of me and help Ashley up. I was glad I parked on the street. Any other time, I would've went straight to the valet. I took her back to the room with me to make sure she was okay and so that she could get her clothes. She wasn't staying with me at all tonight.

"Come on! We have to go!" I yelled at her when I noticed she was done packing her clothes after washing my face and changing my shirt.

"D, who was that girl? Should I be worried?"

"Nobody, but nah. You don't. Just come on. This stays between you and me! Here."

I handed her a stack of money to help ease her mind. I took Ashley back home and headed back to my room. I didn't feel comfortable with her going back home by herself, but I didn't want to run the risk of her getting too attached to me by spending the night. My head was all the way fucked up. Logan really had my shit leaking for a minute. Even though it was against me, I loved and admired the fact that she stood up for herself. I started to blow up her cell phone, but then I remembered I had shattered it when I threw it on the ground. I thought about going past her crib, but I knew that would be a bad idea. I just relaxed and smoked in my room until it was time for me to check out in the morning. I had to pick Dom up at eleven o'clock from the airport. He and Big Rell came back separately just in case we still had eyes on us.

* * *

The next morning, I woke up, and my head was pounding. I tried smoking, and that didn't even help. While I was checking out, I bought an aspirin so that I could drive in peace to go pick Dom up. I had to catch an Uber to pick up my Benz S550 first. I rode the entire way to the airport smoking in my car trying to escape the reality of what I did last night. I pulled up to BWI Airport at the Delta terminal, and Dom was already outside waiting for me.

"What's up, my nigga!" Dom yelled, dapping me up.

"Damn, nigga. You got the dro out early, huh?" he said, looking at the blunt I had in my left hand.

"Man, some shit went down last night," I said, shaking my head.

"Fuck, man. Don't tell me its business related, is it?"

I pulled off.

"Nah, it's me and Lo, man. We got into a fight last night."

"What! A fight? Please tell me you didn't hit her, did you? Rell will kill you!" he asked finally noticing the scratches on my head.

"Yeah, shit got real. You see the scars on my head, nigga!" He started getting on my nerves telling me shit I already knew.

"Man, you gotta help me get Logan back!"

"First Candi, now this shit! Nigga, I'm not a damn therapist!"

"Come on, yo. We brothers! Call Malia real quick and see what she says. Please, yo!"

He called Malia and put her on speaker.

"Hey, baby. You back yet?" Malia asked.

"Yeah, I'm on my way home now. Dre got me. Look, we got a problem."

"Aww shit." She sighed.

"Nah. not on my part. Ya boy Dre needs some relationship help, babe. He did some shit to Logan."

"Dre Dre, what happened?"

"We had a big fight last night, and I hit her."

"Noooo! Never mind. My baby is crying. I will just talk to you when y'all get here. Bye!" She hung up.

"See, nigga you just need to chill, and stop trying to be mister player with these bitches out her. Just settle down with a good woman like Logan before you fuck your life up. But we can't let Brandon or Rell find this out," Dom said.

"Man, you always trying to school me!"

He thought because he was thirty-three that he could always speak his mind to me or something.

"Man, you asking for me and my lady's help, so you're going to hear my mouth regardless."

We rode the rest of the way in silence. We got to Dom and Malia's crib, and they were like the street model couple. They were together for years, and I was sure they had their share of hard times, but they seemed to survive. They had a football team of five kids. The youngest was about three months. They had a nanny and everything in this big ass house out in Laurel, Maryland.

We got to the front door, and all the kids ran up to us, hugging and holding us. All I could hear was "*Daddy... Uncle Dre Dre!*"

We hugged them all and walked in the kitchen where Malia was holding the baby girl they nicknamed "Nook."

"Hey, baby!" Malia said, passing the baby to Dom. He slobbed her down, and all the kids said ewww in the background. It was funny, but I couldn't help but to think of how much I wanted the exact same thing for me and Logan.

"Dre Dre, give me some love. Y'all kiddos go finish playing or watching TV. Y'all don't need to be in grown folks' conversations."

She extended her arms, and I walked over and gave her a hug. Malia was like a big sister I'd never had. It was always just me and my mom.

"So I've been thinking since I got off the phone with y'all that I will call Logan up and ask her to go shopping, then seduce her into coming back here with me. What do y'all think?"

"Hell yeah. That sounds good to me! Me and Dom will just stay here with the kids," I said, excited as shit just at the chance of being able to be around her again. They both burst out laughing at me.

"I will call her and see what she says." Malia pulled out her phone.

"No, babe. This retarded nigga broke her phone last night too!" Dom yelled out. I cut my eyes at him.

"Dre, what the hell else happened? I know for a fact Brandon and Big Rell don't know!"

"Look… long story short, we broke up, and I've been tryna get her ass back, but I caught her out on a date last night while I was with some young chick I had just met. Things led to us outside tussling on the side of the building. Both of us have bad tempers."

Malia shook her head while covering her face. "Got damn, bro! You're really gonna owe me big for this one! You need to park your car in the garage."

"Good idea! Anything for you, sis. Just help a nigga out," I said.

CHAPTER 18

Logan

$\mathcal{I}$ had laid in the bed all day, lying in my own misery. I barely had eaten anything. I was high as hell for hours. I barely got any sleep last night thinking about Dre. I had popped the rest of the Percocets I had left in the prescription bottle. *I'm an RN popping pills now, smh!* I knew the long-term effects they had on people! I needed to get up so I could go to the store and get a new phone. I knew that shit would cost me a lot because I didn't have any kind of protection plan on my service.

I decided to get myself together and get my clothes on. As I was fixing my hair, I heard a knock at my door. *It better not be fucking Dre!* I opened my door, surprised to see Malia.

"Hey, suga!"

She reached out, giving me a hug.

"Hey, Malia. What brings you by? Come on in," I said nervously. She came in sitting at my dining room table.

"So you know I've found out what happened last between you

and Dre. As a woman, I apologize, and I would like for you to come along shopping with me. I know you feel hurt, but you don't need to be in this house cooped up all day, baby girl. You know I've always loved you like a little sister, even your crazy friend Quinn."

We both laughed a bit.

"Yeah, I guess could. I know you drove all the way here from Laurel. Plus, I was getting dressed to go out and get a new phone since Dre's dumbass broke my old one," I said, raising my voice.

"Have you told your parents or Brandon?"

"Hell no," I said quickly.

"Oh okay," she said, chuckling a bit.

"I'm going to finish throwing on my clothes. Give me about ten minutes, and I will be ready."

"Take your time, doll," Malia said.

* * *

We ended up going to Annapolis Mall. I was able to find a few cute clothes, but I was feeling a bit laid back because of the pills wearing off I had taken earlier. Malia was such a cute mom. She pretty much shopped for her kids and only bought one pair of shoes for herself. I was able to get a new phone and keep my number, thank God. On our way back in town, I was catching up on messages from Kelsi and Quinn. I hadn't seen them in over a week. That was long for us. Malia suggested stopping past her house so I could see the kids and the baby. I had a bit of a bad feeling about it, but I didn't want to complain while she had been generous the entire day.

We pulled up to this house, and a weird sensation instantly came over me. Something didn't feel right. Regardless, I had my small gun hiding inside of my purse if some shit went down.

The kids were so cute. I hadn't seen them in months. They went to play in their playroom downstairs in the basement. I could've sworn I heard someone say Dre's name, but I brushed it off. I was sitting in the kitchen, holding the baby while Malia was pulling a cake out she made that she wanted me to taste. She was always a good baker.

"Where's my big brother Dom at?"

As if on cue or some shit, Dom and Dre came up from the basement. Dre came and tried to sit next to me. I immediately got up, giving the baby to Malia and went upstairs to use the bathroom. I was sitting on the toilet, holding back tears. This shit was messed up. I could hear the kids running up the stairs. She must've been getting them to lie down for bed.

"Logan!" I heard Malia knocking on the door. "You okay in there?"

"Yeah! I will be out in a minute!" I yelled.

"Okay, I will be downstairs," Malia said. I wiped my tears. About ten minutes later, I heard fussing coming from downstairs. It was Dom arguing with his first baby mama, Tiara, who was coming to drop off his oldest son that he'd had at a young age unannounced. I noticed Deandre standing off to the side, egging him on and instigating shit as he always did. I stood at the top of the steps and could hear Malia going off on the poor girl to the point where Tiara just got scared and left on her own terms. Malia loved that little boy like her own, but his mother shouldn't have been dropping that child off this late in the evening, especially without warning.

When everything settled down and she left, I took it as my chance to ask Malia if she could she take me home. They all looked at me like I was crazy, like I'd messed up the game plan or something by trying to go home.

"Come on, pooh. Gather your purse so I can get you up the road. I thought I was going to have to kill a bitch in my own house!" she yelled, grabbing her keys and drinking a glass of water. We began walking out.

"What took you so long upstairs, Logan?" Deandre had the nerve to ask me.

"Excuse me? You have no right to question me."

"I just wanted to know if you were feeling okay," he said.

"Don't worry about me!" I cut my eyes at him.

Malia and I walked to open the door, and Dre followed us to the car. Dom just stood back, shaking his head and crossing his arms over his chest. Dre was on my heels as I walked to the passenger side of Malia's Escalade ESV. I tried pulling the door shut, but he stuck his leg in the door and opened it back up with his man strength.

"Move, Dre!" I yelled.

"I just want to talk to you for a moment."

"No! I hate you!" I yelled.

"Logan, come on now! Look, you will always be my wife. Stop playing like this, I fucked up last night!

"No! Leave me alone!" I yelled again, trying to close the door.

Something must've clicked in his brain. He started choking me to the point my head was mashed up against the steering wheel. I couldn't breathe. Tears were falling. I couldn't believe this was happening again for the second night in a row. Malia was trying to pull him off of me but was too short for him to budge.

"Dre, get off of her!"

She was punching him in the back and trying her hardest. Dom came running up, finally pulling Dre off of me. I jumped out of the car like a madwoman and tried to punch him a few times. He stole me in my eye, and it made me want to fight even harder. Dom and Malia were trying their best to stop us, but everybody was winded. I went back to the car to grab my purse. Enough was enough. My life was being threatened too much within the last twenty-four hours.

I pulled my gun out, shooting it in the air, stopping everybody dead in their tracks.

"So now you got a gun, Logan? Huh!" Dre yelled getting himself together. "Since you wanna play so tough, shoot me then!"

I did as I was told and shot toward him.

"Logan!" Malia yelled.

"Fuck! She shot me in the shoulder!" Dre yelled.

"Shit! Shit!" Dom said.

"Logan, get in the car! Dom, take Dre to the hospital or call the team doctor!"

Malia and I hopped in the truck and sped off. *He can take his shot-up shoulder home to his bitch!*

"My goodness, Logan. Are you okay?"

"Yeah, I'm fine. Just get me home, and keep Deandre away from me," I said in between tears.

"I got you, babe. Do you need me to stay with you?"

"No. I am just going to call Quinn or Kelsi to come over," I said dryly. I was numb, deep in thought on the entire ride home. We got back to my condo, and Malia helped me up the stairs. Quinn told me she would be on her way over. I would forever be done with Deandre after tonight. Things had gone completely too far!

I hugged Malia goodbye. She apologized for the thousandth time. I thanked her, and she finally left. I got in the shower and put on some pajamas. Not too long after, Quinn knocked on the door. I was glad she bought food with her. I was so hungry.

"Oh my God, Logan! Dre did this to you?" Quinn asked, examining my face and throat. I still had the scars from yesterday. I even strategically did my makeup so that they wouldn't show on my and Malia's outing today.

I started crying again.

"Yes!"

I started telling her everything that happened between us the last few weeks, and she couldn't believe her ears.

"Logan, I wish I would've known! Ugh, and I need to talk to Malia. I love her dearly, but she was definitely a part of the setup to get you there and have Dre talk to you. It just didn't pan out the way they wanted it to. Dre needs to grow the fuck up! I love him dearly like a brother too. Shit, he even helped with my own personal situation with Fatu, but he can't have his way with you like this."

"I know, Quinn. I really hate him. We started off so well. Now look! I'm realizing that nobody knew about Dre living with a bitch all this time. Nobody would be going this hard for us to be together if they did know, and definitely not my mama, the way she pushed me to ride with him after Kennedy's recital. I will get to the bottom of it eventually, but I will be moving on permanently!" I exclaimed.

"I can't wait to beat that bitch's ass, whoever the hell she is!"

Quinn laughed. We chilled, ate, and watched *Black Ink* reruns for the rest of the night.

CHAPTER 19

Dre

*D*om was flying in his Range Rover supercharged. I wasn't going to any damn hospital. In my eyes, since a gun was involved, that meant I would've had to snitch, and I damn sure wasn't a rat! He drove me to the same doctor we always used for the squad. This was my first time actually going to him. My shoulder was leaking, and it was hot as hell. I kept smelling the whiff of my flesh burning. I couldn't even be mad at Lo though. She was my baby forever. I was mad she had shot me in the same shoulder I had already been shot in years ago. I had to really pay attention to what this doctor was going to tell me.

On some real shit, I couldn't even explain the level of how low I felt. I couldn't do shit but blame myself. I had to be honest. It was my entire fault. I wanted Logan back so bad that I didn't know how to still respect her when she would stand up for herself by pushing me away. All along, she was just naturally trying to protect herself. Shit had gotten way out of control. I guess at this point, I needed to keep my distance. Unfortunately, I would have to go back to my safe zone. *Candi!*

I wasn't telling anybody this shit. It would have to stay between the people who were there, and of course, I couldn't hide it from my mama, I would just tell her it happened in the streets. It was time for me to lay low and keep building this empire up. Dom and I still had unfinished business to handle, manning down these streets.

* * *

Logan

It took me about a week to recover from the crazy events of me and Deandre, but I was holding on strong. The good thing was that I was able to concentrate more at work and finishing my semester for school in good standing. It had been about two months since everything transpired. I heard through the grapevine (Malia) that Dre had gotten locked up on a gun charge for getting pulled over with a gun in the car. So of course, he was now fighting a case for not only that, but it also went hand in hand with violating his probation, his worst fear, which it seemed to happen to a lot of young black men these days. Malia told me Dom bonded him out immediately, and he was awaiting his trial. God bless him, but I was too blessed to be stressed at the moment. I was a young woman with her shit together. I didn't have time to argue with a nigga all day.

Brandon was finally beginning to open up. He finally started calling me every day. I had plans to take Kennedy with me to see him within the following weeks. I was still two seconds from wanting to kill Shay's ass. My pops made her move out of the house and took the cars back her and Brandon were sharing. She was mad as hell, but shit, why would she need to hold on to shit that my brother footed the bill on while she had a new man. She was lucky he didn't give a fuck about her salon and chucked it up as a loss for the sake of Kennedy. Brandon was also still waiting on sentencing. Murder trials always were so drawn out to me. I still hadn't said anything to him or my father about me and Dre falling out so badly. Way too much blood would have been shed behind it. I just let them think we went our separate ways peacefully.

I had gone out on a few more dates with Derrick. He was growing on me a bit, but he knew I wasn't looking for a relationship. I was sure he was still doing him, which I was cool with. I hadn't given him the cookie at all anyway. He would annoy me trying to figure out where I lived and kept asking when he could come over, but I always shot him down. I met him wherever we went out at. Still, nobody at work knew we were dating except for Kelsi. He would send me flowers and lunch to my charge desk with "Your Admirer" written on it. He was a nice guy, but God knew deep inside I had a thing for them street niggas. Shit, look at my damn daddy.

Tonight was my mom's fiftieth birthday party that we had been planning for a while now. I was in my kitchen, putting the finishing touches on my special seafood salad I liked to make. I had to back out of making the entire menu for the party. Between school and work, I couldn't find the time to be able to prepare all of that food and find the help in order to cater it correctly. It would've been too many people in the room that I would've been trying to impress that my dad was doing business with. I hoped Deandre didn't end up coming.

I had to get ready quickly when I was done and bring my dress to the venue with me. I got in the shower and did my makeup, but I left my hair in the flexi rods to hold my curls intact. Me having to play the role of responsible daughter, I was helping the event planner with setup. My mom was very picky, and I wanted her night to be one to remember. I had a red carpet and two photo booths set up for her as a surprise. I wished Quinn could have made it, but she was in New York visiting family this weekend, and the job wouldn't approve Kelsi for the night off.

Dre

I went to my mom's house to pick her up so that we could go to Mama Tricey's party together. My shoulder had heeled up pretty well so far, and I was able to get my cast off last week. Lately, I had been staying with her more often because Candi was getting on my nerves per usual. It was crazy because she always threatened calling my PO, and I ended up getting myself in trouble anyway. She now realized she couldn't get to me in that way anymore since I was in trouble now. I was trying to lay low while fighting my cases. I was still fucking Ashley's little naïve ass from time to time. But Logan was always on my mind.

My mother gave me a pep talk before we walked in the party. She wanted me back with Logan just as much as I wanted to be. She told me she had heard Logan was seeing some guy. I knew one thing, I better not have seen him tonight. My mom kept saying my spirit had changed since Logan and I weren't on speaking terms.

We walked in the party, greeting everyone. I started seeing people there I hadn't seen since my dad died. They even had an area set up with photos for loved ones who had passed away over the last fifty years. My ghetto ass mother begged me to take a picture of her standing next to my father's picture. We had been there for about an hour before I noticed Logan. We locked eyes from across the room while the photographer took pictures of her helping her mother cut the big ass cake. I didn't see my Kennedy running around, so I assumed she must not have been allowed. Shay had hit me up a few days ago asking to borrow ten stacks. That bitch had lost her mind. She should've thought about that shit before she disowned my bro like that. I sat at a table, scanning the room and stealing glances of Logan.

Logan

I saw Dre sitting at a table toward the back of the room. He looked nice.

"Why don't you take your ass over there and just say hello to him," my mom whispered in my ear. She must've noticed who I was looking at. I started laughing to myself as she walked off. *Whelp... here goes a try.* If I didn't do it now, I would be uncomfortable the entire party. I decided to take the scenic route over to him.

"Hey, Dre Dre. How are you?" I asked, sitting down next to him and yelling over the Baltimore house music the DJ was blasting in the background. He didn't see me coming.

"Hey, Lo Lo. You're looking beautiful as always," he said, scanning my body up and down. I had on a beautiful solid blue off the shoulder peplum mermaid style dress with gold accessories, which matched the party décor. Just then, his mom came over giving me a hug. I could smell the Crown Royal on her breath. That was Mama Pam for you.

"There goes my baby! My Logie Lo. Why haven't you come over? I miss you, girl. When are you and Dre gonna get this shit together and give me some grandbabies, huh?"

"Ma, chill. That's enough. Why don't you go back over there and dance or something? Damn," he said, getting annoyed. I felt bad for him a bit. I knew he always hated how lit his mom would get.

"Oh shut the hell up, Dre. Bye, Logan, baby. We will finish this conversation when the party is over."

She walked away, doing her old head two step. We laughed at her and then looked back at one another.

"I miss you a lot, Logan!"

He stared in my eyes, searching for a physical response.

"I can't say that I don't miss you, but sometimes a woman has to walk away from what she loves in order to get what she deserves."

He nodded, not liking my response and continuing to eat his food.

"I guess I will see you around sometime."

I began getting up, but he pulled me back down.

"Look… let's get out of here and go talk." I started to say no, but something told me to say yes.

We left out of the beautiful World Trade Center building and began walking and talking around the harbor like we were getting to know one another all over again. It felt so good outside in the beautiful summer breeze. I realized that at one time in my life, he was beginning to be my best friend. We literally were eating each meal together as one every day. I had to be honest with myself and admit I knew he was a hurt man on the inside. All of the signs were there. He was clearly insecure and constantly felt low about himself, which caused him to lash out physically. He was never taught the healthy way to channel his anger properly, and him being a boss in the streets fueled his egotistical personality, making matters much worse. But it wasn't my job to teach a man how to be a man. I could push him to do it, but it was up to him to make the change.

"Logan, let's escape reality tonight. We can't go back in the party though. They will try to make us stay."

"Yeah, you have a good point. Where are you trying to go to?"

"Let's hit Atlantic City."

"Atlantic City? I'm not driving there this time of night!" I said, getting loud.

"Come on now, Logan. Don't disrespect me like that. You know I will treat and drive up there."

"What about clothes?" I asked.

"We will buy everything when we get there. Let's go."

I got him to follow me in order to park my car at my house, and I ran upstairs to change my clothes and pack a bag. Shoot, I wasn't paying him any mind. I liked to be prepared, even if it was just a one-night ordeal. I sent my mom a long text, asking her to take Mama Pam home for Dre, and I told her the truth, explaining everything that happened. She took a while to reply back, which I expected, but I was sure she was happy I was actually speaking to Deandre.

CHAPTER 20

Dre

I was excited as hell to be around Logan again. I thought she was going to deny me, honestly. We made the two-hour journey up the highway to A.C. and paying all of them tolls was a bitch. I held Logan's hand the entire ride, even though she had fallen asleep for most of it. I knew she'd had a long day, so I didn't bother her. I pulled my G-Wagon up to the Borgata Hotel & Casino. It was a few blocks over from the boardwalk, but it was spacious and new. I woke Logan up and grabbed her bag from the backseat. I kept eyeballing her the whole ride. She was my baby, and I had fucked up bad. We walked hand in hand to our room. I always got some type of luxury suite in whatever hotel I ever stayed in. I waited for Logan to change her clothes in the room while I went downstairs to the Hugo Boss store inside the hotel to get myself a few outfits.

When I was done, I went back upstairs to get Logan, and she looked like a fucking snack in the all-white dress she had put on. We went to walk around the casino area, and I began shooting craps on the table game. Logan must've been my good luck charm because I was winning, rolling fives back to back. I gave Logan some money to get on the slot machines adjacent to the table and even she started hitting big. We got drinks at the bar, and we started reminiscing even more as we sat there drinking. One thing I loved about Logan was that she always had a listening ear. I told her about my legal problems, and she just kept saying how much the Lord would bring me through it.

We ended up going back to the room, tired as hell. It was about 4 a.m. by that time. Logan sat down on the bed, removing her shoes. I stood there admiring her. Then, in one swift move, I pushed her further on the bed, pulling her underwear down her legs, and dove in her pussy head first. She began screaming and grabbing my head, and we started fucking like rabbits. I think we both had a lot of tension built up.

She pushed me off of her while I was hitting her from the side, making me sit down on the bed. She got down on her knees and swallowed my entire ruler sized dick in her mouth. I had to admit that I loved when she got drunk. She wasn't so innocent anymore. She was giving me head so good that I felt myself sliding off the bed. I loved the fact that she let me pull on her hair, but I knew not to push her head down to hard. I nutted long and hard. She got up, sitting on my dick, and my dick got hard again inside of her. We continued fucking for another hour until we both were exhausted. We barely made it up in time for check out. I woke up to Logan's fake ass lashes lying in front of me on the pillow. All I could do was laugh. We walked the boardwalk after we checked out of the room and found a spot to eat breakfast.

As we made our way back to Baltimore, I couldn't help but to think how much I wanted to be there for Logan in so many ways, but deep down inside, I knew I couldn't.

Now, I was in the situation of trying to prepare myself for jail time. I knew sooner or later my lawyer wouldn't be able to keep postponing the courts, and I would have to turn myself in. On top of it all, I was still living with Candi because of my fear of losing everything. It was like everything I was scared of losing that I kept trying to control was being pulled right from up under me anyway, so I might as well just let shit go. I think a part of me liked being able to get over on Candi in ways that I couldn't do with Logan, which fed my ego even more.

I dropped Logan off at her building, fearing that this would be my last time seeing her for a while. We gave each other a long hug, and we went our separate ways.

Logan

*D*amn, I didn't want to leave from out of Dre's arms. It was crazy how funny life was. You loved somebody with all your soul, and then God allowed that same person to reveal themselves as not being good for you. The same red flags that you ignored in the beginning would be the same reason it all ended. How could any of us evolve and grow to be better if we just settled for our comfort zones? The spirit of fear was the trick of the enemy. Time was too precious, and life was way too short. If a blessing was directly in your face, you must be sure to take advantage of it. I was a true believer in carpe diem! That was exactly why I knew I would have to keep my distance from Dre; even through all the love we shared, there was still a wall he held up that he wasn't ready to break down. I would not be there to tolerate the disrespect while he figured his life out. Maybe this friendship thing could work, but only time would tell.

* * *

A few weeks later, I decided to go pick up Kennedy. I still hadn't talked to Dre since our short getaway. Kennedy and I hadn't spent as much time together since my mother had been picking her up on the regular for me. Brandon had finally gotten sentenced and began his prison term. He and I decided to keep it a secret that I was bringing her to see him today. I definitely didn't want to tell Dre. He would've been asking too many questions that I wouldn't have felt like answering. Besides, the visit was about Kennedy, and I knew that he and Brandon talked damn near every day through my father's phone.

We pulled up to the jail, and Kennedy started rolling with the questions.

"Auntie, where are we? I see police!"

"We're here to see someone special, Ken."

"Who?" she asked, eating her last few French fries.

"It's a surprise."

We made it past the security check. Kennedy was mad she had to throw away the rest of her Happy Meal like I didn't warn her five times. So when we walked in the visitation room and she saw the vending machines, she ran directly to them, pointing to exactly what she wanted. *Gosh, this child is spoiled!* While she was waiting for the snacks to fall, I noticed Brandon walking in sitting at the table they assigned for us.

"Look, Ken. There goes Daddy!"

She turned around, and when she realized it was Brandon, she hauled ass toward him. I had to catch her before we got kicked out before our visit even started. I went back to grab her snacks and held her hand, walking toward the table.

"Daddy! Daddy!" She jumped up on him. It was a bittersweet moment. I began to tear up a little. He put her down and reached in to hug me.

"What's up, sis?"

"Bro, I missed you! You're looking healthy!" We hugged and sat down.

"Daddy, I missed you this much!" She opened her arms wide, grinning. Kennedy had the same high cheekbones and chinky eyes that I did.

"No. I missed you this much!" Brandon said, opening his long arms wide.

"Y'all are silly." I laughed at them.

"So, sis, what's going on with you and Dre?"

"Damn, Brandon. Why you gotta start off digging so deep?" I rolled my eyes.

"Man, just answer the question?" He chuckled, mushing me in the face.

"We are just friends for now."

"Yeah, aight. I will find out the truth. You can't hide forever, Lo." He kept laughing.

"Daddy, I don't like Mommy's new boyfriend!" Kennedy butted in.

"Oh really? Daddy will handle it."

"I want to stay with Mi Mi and Pop Pop or Auntie."

"We will work it out as soon as y'all leave here. Don't worry, baby girl. Even though I will be here for a while, I still have things under control for you," Brandon said seriously.

The sad part was I knew exactly what he really meant about what he was saying to Ken. We stayed there for two hours, and Kennedy started giving me a hard time once she realized we were leaving. The guards gave us an extra fifteen minutes to give Brandon a chance to calm her down. The more we came, the better it would help her understand her dad wasn't leaving her forever. Our dad planned on paying a few lawyers and judges off to get an appeal for him in order to minimize his sentence. Given the circumstances of the family business, Brandon only had a bad juvenile record, he had never been locked up as an adult, so that would help a lot.

On my way back home, Kennedy was passed out in the backseat. I noticed my phone ringing with "Unknown" as the caller ID. I ignored it until the person kept calling back to back. Becoming irritated, I answered it with an attitude.

"Lola Bunny!"

"Dre?"

"Yeah it's me! Why do you sound mad?"

"Why in the hell are you calling me blocked?" I shot back at him.

"I didn't think you would answer if I called you from one of my regular numbers."

"Shit, Dre. You're lucky my curiosity allowed me to pick it up just now!"

"Anyway, what are you doing? I would like to see you this evening!"

I paused feeling confused since we hadn't talked in a while. "Ummm, nothing, actually. I am about to drop Kennedy off at my parents' and then head home."

"Do you mind if I meet you at your house?"

I thought about it. *Shit, why not.* Letting my guard down for some reason, I said, "Yeah, I should be home around 7:00."

"Okay, bet. I will see you then, baby mama."

"Bye, Dre!" I sounded annoyed and hung up.

CHAPTER 21

Dre

I was in the house relaxing while Candi was at work. Ever since we came back from Atlantic City, I knew I needed to make a change, and quick. I called Logan from a blocked number because I didn't want her to feel free enough to call me anytime, especially if I was home with Candi, even though she hadn't called me. I knew it was a fucked up way of thinking, but I had to keep all my ducks in a row. I wanted to see her badly. On one hand, I wanted to let her be and allow her to enjoy her life knowing she didn't deserve this shit. On the other hand, I couldn't let any other nigga have a chance at getting at her the way I had. I couldn't leave too much space between us for her to think she was getting over me and moving on to someone else. Until I was ready to fully commit to her, I didn't see anything wrong with sliding back from her when I felt I needed to.

I got myself together and left out of the house heading toward Logan's place. Dom called me saying he and Malia were planning to go to the strip club tonight. Those two sure knew how to keep their relationship going. He asked did I want to come along, but I told him I would get back at him about it.

I pulled up at Logan's house and parked in the visitor's space next to the truck I gave her. It was dirty as shit. She knew how I felt about dirty cars. When I got to her door and she opened it, I couldn't help but to admire how beautiful she was.

"Dre..." She snapped at me.

I was in a trance. I shook my head. "Shit, my bad."

She giggled. "You good?"

"Yeah, I just love you. What's up with the Mazi truck?" I looked serious.

"What you mean? I drove it earlier."

"It's dirty as shit on the outside."

"You promised me you would keep it up, and now we're never around each other, so it's your fault," she said, laughing.

"Dom and Malia are going out tonight, we got invited. Are you trying to come?"

"I would say no, but knowing you, you won't take no for answer any way." She shook her head.

"You've always been a smart girl and have always had a good memory." I laughed slapping her on the ass as she walked in the kitchen.

"Watch your hands, sir," she yelled.

"I can touch anything that belongs to me," I said, getting up giving her a hug from behind.

"Nigga, you're lucky I even let you come over," she said, rolling her eyes. "Get off of me and go watch TV or something, I need to start my dinner." She pushed me out of the kitchen.

Logan knew I loved her cooking. "I want something fried!" I yelled while flipping through the channels on the television.

"You are going to eat whatever I cook!" she yelled back.

She was always timing up for my ass. I loved how she always stood up for herself. We ate her famous spaghetti with shrimp inside. I ate so much I fell asleep on the couch as I waited for her to get dressed. We hopped in the Mazi truck, and I went to the 24-hour carwash at the gas station just to get it clean real quick. I couldn't be seen getting out of something that wasn't clean.

I pulled up to On the Block located on Baltimore Street, which was the famous block full of strip clubs galore. Dom and Malia were waiting for us inside the club. I still hadn't told Malia exactly where we were going. I parked the car and checked my phones.

"You meeting somebody down here or something?" Logan asked.

"Nope. Come on; let's get out. They're waiting on us."

"Since when have we gone to strip clubs together?" she asked getting out.

"Since now." I grabbed her hand as we walked toward the club.

I dapped up the bouncers when we got to the door, and Logan looked at me shaking her head. I hoped this night would roll over well. I spotted Malia at the bar first, and she walked us to the section they already had blocked off for us.

Logan

Dre was funny as hell for bringing me here. What he didn't know was that I was completely comfortable being here. Malia, Quinn, and I used to come all the time. A few of the girls I still recognized. It's weird because I had never been to a male strip club, they all seemed a bit gay to me. But tonight, I wasn't tipping anybody more than the twenty ones that were already in my pocket.

"Hey, suga. How have you been?" The stripper named Honey came over to me, giving me a hug. Dre and Dom were looking dumbfounded at first. They were so preoccupied by a group of girls that had surrounded them in a pile while they were throwing stacks of ones at them.

"I've been good, babe. Can you do me a favor?" I asked Honey.

"Anything for you." She sat next to me.

"Can you give my good friend over there a lap dance?" I asked, pointing to Dre, and Malia started dying laughing.

"Of course."

I grabbed her hand and walked toward Dre, excusing myself between the other dancers. He looked at me confused. I think he was scared that I was beginning to get upset with the atmosphere. I softly pulled Honey from behind me and sat her on Dre's lap. I whispered in her ear, "I am going to get you some real cash tonight." She smiled and gave Dre a lap dance that I knew he would remember for years. Malia, Dom, and I stood around throwing ones, watching, and cracking up at his facial expressions. When Honey was done, we gave each other a high five, cracking up, and she went back to making her rounds around the rest of the club. Dre was all smiles. He and I sat on the couch next to Dom and Malia.

"Damn, babe, did you know her or some shit?" he asked, leaning in close to me.

"I sure did," I said smiling.

"You lying!"

"She's not lying, Dre," Malia said laughing.

We finished up our night having fun with the strippers and drinking. Dre decided to be a copycat and sent Honey over to me for a friendly lap dance as a joke while everyone stood around recording. I even, at one point, got up next to her and started twerking, but Dre didn't let that last past two minutes.

We eventually left the club and went to a late-night diner called Sip N Bite. While we were eating our food, a fight broke out at the table across from us. It was a group full of girls that looked to be friends at first, from what I could tell. Somebody said "...*you fucked my nigga*..." and it was on from there. The chicks started throwing silverware and glass cups around. Dom and Dre started instigating the situation, making me and Malia mad. When one girl went to grab a chair, I had, had enough. *It was time to go!* We packed our shit and dipped. The fight broke out just in time because we had all just finished eating, and I would be damned if any of us paid the bill.

Dre and I were riding toward the direction of my house, listening to some 90's slow jams. I was cracking up at his non-singing ass trying to sing to me and still drive. He pulled over abruptly a few minutes later on the side of Key Highway.

"What's wrong?" I looked concerned.

He grabbed my left hand and looked me in my eyes. "I love you, Logan. You really mean a lot to me. I would be a dumbass nigga if I really didn't wife you completely when this case shit is all over. I really want us to move in together. You are really the one. I want you to be my wife and the mother of my kids. Shit, we just went to the strip club as a couple, and you even sent a girl to me. Not too many women can handle shit like that. I admire your confidence and strength. I know I've been a fucked up nigga to you, but I want to move past my wrongs."

"Damn, Dre, that was unexpected. I don't know what to say."

"You don't have to say anything." He grabbed my face and tongue kissed me.

He stopped. "Get in the back seat."

"Huh?"

"Get in the back seat," he repeated.

I climbed over the armrest in the backseat, accidentally hitting Dre in the head with my heel.

"Damn, Lo Lo." He held his forehead.

I chuckled covering my mouth. "My bad, Dre Dre!"

He got out of the driver's side pulling down the backseats exposing the trunk. My drunk ass wasn't catching on to what he was trying to do at first, until he pulled off my shoes and skirt before I could object. Dre pulled me down on my back and ate my damn pussy with no type of remorse. I could tell I started squeezing his face too hard with my thighs, but I couldn't help it, and he seemed not to care. Every time I tried grabbing his head or ears, he would lock my hands with his and hold them over my head, which made me scream even louder than I already was. He pulled out his dick, ramming it inside of me, causing me to dig my nails in his back. Drunken sex was the best sex. We went at it for a few more minutes until Dre's paranoid ass saw some police lights riding by and a few people walking past made him slow down and stop.

"Why you stop?" I said out of breath.

"I'm out on bail, Lo. Let's finish this in the house," he said, staring out of the window.

"Ughhhh." I huffed crossing my arms.

I stayed in the back as he got himself together and drove to my house. We fucked between the kitchen counter and the living room the remainder of the night. We got in the bed and held each other the remainder of the night. It was sad how much love we shared, and things never went all the way right with us. My gut was still telling me he was hiding something from me.

CHAPTER 22

Dre

$\mathcal{I}$t felt 100% right being with Logan. I was going to step out on faith and follow my heart. I was miserable with Candi from the beginning. I never even parked every car I had at that house. I rented a garage space in a location nobody but Dom and Brandon knew about to store my cars. Candi only knew of me having the S550 Benz, which was my everyday car that everyone around the city knew me by. She didn't even know about the G-Wagon I had. I didn't care what Logan said, we were going to move into the house in Pennsylvania whether she liked it or not. I had been paying rent on that house for months, and it sat empty. Eventually, I planned on me and Logan finding a different house that we would be able to buy together once I served my jail time.

The next morning, I woke up on a mission. It was Sunday, and I knew Candi was gone to church with her mother. For some reason, even though she was a stripper, she seemed to still be able to keep up with going to church and never missed a Sunday since I have known her the last few years. I got out of the bed without waking Logan. I went to the house me and Candi shared and packed all of my shit up. I was done. I knew Logan would be happy.

I decided to leave all of my clothes and shoes I packed in the car. When I made it back to Logan's place, she looked irritated when she opened the door for me.

"You thought I was gone for good, didn't you?" I laughed at her attitude.

"It's not funny," she yelled, hitting me on the back.

"I gotta surprise for you this afternoon," I said.

"What?" She looked excited, changing her mood quickly.

"I said it's a surprise, crazy! Go put some clothes on, wear something sexy and casual."

"Dre, that doesn't even make sense."

"You'll figure it out."

"Ugh!" She stomped off. I heated up some of the spaghetti she made last night.

Logan

I walked in my closet, trying to figure out what the hell to wear. I ended up putting on a tight fitting red maxi style dress I got from Fashion Nova and paired it with my nude Valentino flip-flops. *I wondered where this crazy nigga was taking me. He had too many surprises good and bad.*

We hopped in the car and got on the highway. It looked like we were heading toward Route 50. Twenty-five minutes later, we looked to have arrived in Annapolis, Maryland. We pulled up to Carrol's Creek Café located on the waterfront. We got a few stares being that we were the only black couple in the restaurant. *Fuck them.*

"How did you find this place?"

"Google," Dre said, laughing.

"Aw, I'm proud of you, Dre Dre. You're really trying."

"I want better, and the first thing is getting you back all the way."

"Shit, you should've been gotten in trouble, if it's making you act this way." We chuckled.

"Naaaah, whatever happens with my case, I swear this would be my last time going to jail. I'm twenty-seven. A nigga is tired. And with Brandon gone, I can't leave Dom and your dad out here by themselves but for so long. Plus, we got kids to make. I nutted in you real good at least three times last night."

I burst out laughing. "You always know how to ruin a good conversation!"

He laughed. "I'm serious though, Lola Bunny. All jokes aside, you were around when my dad died. You know me and my mother went through a lot, which only caused me to go harder in the streets. I used to ride up and down Penn North on a damn bike selling loud all day, getting high off my own supply, being dumb until your dad stepped in taking me under his wing. You know Pam was denying help big time back then."

I teared up a bit. Dre wanted to love so badly, but he was so hurt on the inside. And now he's at the age where his money and greed has gotten the best of him. He was confused, still trying to figure out life and was taking the wrong roots to gain stability. What type of person would allow himself or herself to go home every night to a person they hated for years but had the money and opportunity to leave; a person who still had a hurt child inside of them. I always said when I had kids, I prayed I would be able to raise my kids to become healthy adults that wouldn't have to live their adult lives recovering from their childhood. I know Momma Pam did her best given the situation back then, but she shouldn't have run through men the way she did in front of Deandre. That's another reason I knew deep down inside he didn't trust women because of the men his mom brought in and out.

We ate our brunch, and Dre dropped two one-hundred-dollar bills on the table to cover the bill. We went to walk around the waterfront at the restaurant. A white woman stopped us as we walked hand in hand.

"I must say you two make a fine looking young, Black couple. I don't get to see your type that often." My first reaction was to beat that bitch's ass right there on the spot, but I felt Dre gripping my hand tightly.

"Thanks, miss," he said.

"Why didn't you let me slap that old white hoe?" I yelled.

"She wasn't worth it!"

I looked at him shocked. I put the back of my hand on his forehead. "You okay? What's really going on with you?"

"I'm good, Logan. I just have a lot on my mind today." He kissed me.

We finally headed toward the car and headed back up the rode home.

"Dre, what's all of that in the back seat?"

"All my shit. Are you going to put it away for me?"

"Huh, what you mean?"

"It's all of my belongings." He grabbed my hand and kissed it.

"You're moving in my place?" My eyes got big.

"Yup!"

"Oh my gosh, Dre!" I screamed, jumping up in the seat kissing him.

We got to the house and unloaded the car, taking his stuff upstairs. This nigga had more Jordans than Michael Jordan himself. I got tired and left him to finish getting his shit. When he finished, we both relaxed on the couch. I had my laptop in my lap so I could finish my homework assignment that was due by midnight.

"I'm proud of you, Lo Lo. You've really been focused on school and your business plans. I will be giving you your startup money whenever you are ready."

"Dre, no, I can't let you do that. We just got to the point where you are able to really move in."

"Lo, don't disrespect me like that. I am your man, and I am in a position to help you, so I will. I believe in your dream."

I teared up a little. "That means a lot coming from you. I don't know what has gotten into you, but I'm loving this shit. These are the things we have always talked about." We shared a long kiss.

"I think we should take a little trip to celebrate us being official," he said.

"To where?"

"My favorite city, Miami! Look up some rooms and flights for this week, and book it on your card, and I will give you the money to put back on the card. And you know we can't stay more than two days because of my bail."

I chuckled. "Okay!"

He got up and went into the room to take a nap, I assumed.

CHAPTER 23

Dre

$\mathcal{M}$iami was one of my favorite places to visit. This would be my first time coming here not on business. Being with Logan permanently for the last few days has been more peaceful than I expected it to be. Candi had been blowing my shit up, to the point I didn't even turn the phone on that she knew the number to, I always left that shit dead in my glove compartment. Knowing I was facing jail time had my mind all over the place. I was becoming nervous as to whether or not Logan would really stick by me.

Logan and I were sitting across from one another as we ate lunch at Prime 112 on Ocean Drive. She found us an Airbnb located in The Continuum building toward the bottom of Ocean Drive. The apartment was nice as shit. Everything was all white from the walls to the furniture and bedding. Logan was in the process of stuffing her face without any shame, I couldn't help but to laugh at her.

"What are you laughing at?" She rolled her neck looking at me annoyed.

"You, fat girl," I said still laughing.

"Look, you know what it was when you first decided to go after me," she said, hitting the side of her right thigh.

"You know my momma is really happy that you are giving me another chance."

"Dre! You weren't supposed to tell her all of our business!" she whined.

"You know she loves you. It's not like I have any other siblings."

She was eating the chef's grilled salmon entrée and the sweet and spicy chicken wings on the side. I had to be on my big boy shit and ordered a twelve-ounce filet mignon with garlic mashed potatoes and cornbread stuffing. I ate the way I wanted on vacation. I had the money to eat the way I wanted when I wanted. Once we were done, we decided to head toward the beach. That sun in Miami wasn't a joke. I rented a cabana for us to relax in.

I was laid out completely on my back, and Logan laid on my right side with my arm wrapped around her shoulder. I couldn't help but to continuously think about how much I had fucked Logan over. I didn't deserve her. The things I had done to her, if I had a daughter, I would have beat and killed my own ass. I just prayed that she would continue to keep it from her family.

"Do you really love me?" I asked.

"Yes, Dre, why?"

"Because I need to know."

"Stop asking me questions you already know the answer to."

"Are you cheating on me?"

"Dre!" she yelled, sitting up.

"Just answer my question."

"You're beginning to ruin the mood. No I am not cheating!"

Out of nowhere, in usual Florida fashion, it began to rain hard as shit. *Damn, maybe I did ruin the mood.* I grabbed her hand and we took off in the direction of the building we were staying in.

Later that night, we acted like real tourist and walked up and down Ocean Drive bar hopping. Our last spot was at Wet Willie's. Logan and I had three Call A Cab frozen drinks and ended up taking an Uber back to our rental apartment since Logan kept complaining she couldn't feel her legs anymore. While we were in the Uber, I noticed my phone going off.

Unknown: Since you want to leave and ignore me. I got something for ur ass...

Me: Fuck u

I already knew it had to be Candi. How she figured out my other phone number was beyond me, but fuck it, she knew what time it was. *I already packed my shit and left, what more could I do?* Logan was my world, and I was determined to make shit official between us. Candi needed to just move on at this point. I wished we had the opportunity to stay in Miami a bit longer, but I had to rush back to Baltimore because of business and me not really supposed to be leaving the state of Maryland under my probation terms. Logan was my real partner in life. We both were always down to drop everything and skip town. When we got back to the apartment, we fell straight out on the couch, we didn't even make it to the bedroom. We didn't even have sex. Our chemistry was so strong, it was beginning to feel like as a man, I didn't need validation from fucking the shit out of her all the time. That was some real shit because a lot of niggas never even had that feeling with a woman they had been with for years.

The next morning, I woke up looking for my phone, I heard my text message tone going off.

Ashley: I'm pregnant.

Me: Ain't mine what you telling me for...

Ashley started calling me back to back after my reply. She must've not liked what I said. How was she pregnant by me, and we always used condoms? I woke Logan up. I had to admit anytime shit was crazy in my life, I leaned on her for my emotional support because I didn't know how to deal with my emotions properly. We got up and took a bath together in the tub that was adjacent to the floor to ceiling windows with the curtains drawn wide open. I was behind her as she laid her head on my chest. She seemed a little off physically ever since we got off the plane.

"Are you ready to go jet skiing?" I asked her. She still looked half sleep.

"I'm not sure, I'm feeling a bit sluggish, and I keep feeling light headed."

"My twins are on the way!"

"Twins! What twins?"

"The twins that are forming in your stomach right now!" I rubbed her belly.

"Oh hell no, Dre. It's too soon for that. We aren't even all the way right just yet!"

"So you denying me now?" I got serious and sat up. I didn't even mean to yell at her the way I did. I still had that Ashley text on my mind.

"No! Calm down! I just want things to be as perfect as much as they possibly can get."

"Come on, let's just finish washing up so we can get going. My bad, baby." I kissed her.

We finished washing up and got dressed. We caught an Uber to the dock location where the Jet Ski rentals were. The entire ride, Logan had her shades on, and she had her head leaned on my shoulder.

"Logan, we don't have to go if you're not up for it," I said.

"I think I will just sit on the side and watch you have fun."

"That isn't going to be any fun, Lo Lo!"

"It will for me just watching you." She kissed my cheek.

We got to the place and I picked out the Jet Ski I wanted, it was money green. Logan stayed on the sideline recording me going back and forth speeding through the waves. I stayed out on the course for about forty-five minutes, and it started drizzling, so they made our group come back in. When I got back on the dock and was done turning back in the life vest, I noticed Logan slumped over the ramp throwing up. I ran up to her rubbing her back.

"Lo, you good?" She kept throwing up, holding her index finger to me.

"Baby, we gotta get back home. I know we had another day here, but I don't feel right being down here with you not feeling good," I said.

"I'm sorry, Dre." She finally stopped, and I pulled her up in a bear hug.

"It's cool, baby. Let's go back to the apartment and pack."

We got back to the apartment and couldn't find a flight to get us back for this evening. So I had to call Big Rell and get him to charter a jet for us.

* * *

We got back in Baltimore that night and went straight back to the condo. We were lying in the bed watching TV.

"Lo, you need to take a pregnancy test."

"No, I probably only have a stomach bug or something from that food down there."

"Why you keep denying my baby, Lo? I don't like that shit." She sighed, ignoring me. Her phone started ringing, and she looked at it, rolling her eyes and ignored it. Then whoever it was, texted her.

"Who's that?" I asked.

"Nobody."

I grabbed her phone.

Derrick: Hey beautiful its been a while...I hope everything is cool

"So you are fucking this clown ass nigga?" I yelled.

"What? No, Dre, I haven't talked to him in forever."

I snatched her up, choking her a bit. "Are you fucking lying to me?" I yelled at her. She looked scared as shit.

"No, Dre! Let me go! I don't have any energy!"

"Logan, you are about to have me out here bodying this nigga. You bet not be fucking him, or I will kill the both of y'all. You know I am good for it."

"Dre, please calm down!"

I let her go. I went out in the living room and sparked a blunt, leaving Logan in the room.

Me: Wyd

Ashley: Missing you...

Me: I will come see you tomorrow

Ashley: Yes please

CHAPTER 24

Logan

$\mathcal{I}$ felt like shit the entire trip to Miami. I was happy about me and Deandre trying to work things out. I was beginning to notice how much his temper was beginning to get out of control. While I had the day off and Dre was out handling business this afternoon, I mustered up the strength to hit Quinn up to see if she wanted to do some shopping or get a bite to eat.

"Lo Lo!" Quinn yelled through the phone.

"I'm back, what are you doing when you get off? I need to see your face!"

"I thought you were coming back tonight. We can go grab something to eat later on, as long as you're not being held hostage."

I laughed at her comment. "I got sick while we were there, so I came back last night."

"Aw, poor baby. Let's go to Sullivan's," she suggested.

"That's cool. We can meet there at six."

"Okay, babe, see you then. Bye."

After we hung up, I turned on my music, blasting my Xscape station on Pandora, and I started cleaning and putting away some of Dre's clothes he had left around the bedroom. He was such a man, leaving me to put away his clothes. I guess I was officially a housewife now. We agreed to not tell anyone just yet that we moved in together, except for Dom and Malia. They were the only ones we trusted enough to know all of our relationship business. I cleaned the house from top to bottom. Dre hadn't called me all day, and I honestly didn't mind because his moody ass got on my nerves last night. I heard him trying to wake me up this morning when he was leaving, and I pretended to be incoherent. I couldn't believe he yoked me up like that last night. He is lucky I wasn't feeling good. I hoped I wasn't really pregnant. I know most women these days would be flattered to be pregnant by a guy like him, but I wanted my foundation to be solid with whoever the father of my kids would be. By the time I was done, I looked at the clock and it was 5:00 p.m. I hopped in my BMW and rode in the direction of Sullivan's so that I could meet Quinn.

I walked in and spotted Quinn sitting in a booth a few feet back from the door. She jumped up and squealed. She was always dramatic.

"Bestie, I missed you!" she yelled, hugging me.

"I know, babe, we've never gone this long without physically seeing each other!"

"I blame Dre's ass! He probably done moved in and everything."

I gave her the dick look. "He did move in the other day."

"Bitch, stop playing! Logan, you are holding back, boo, I should come across the table and beat your ass, bitch! And why do you look like you're glowing?"

"I don't know, I told you I was sick in Miami."

"Oh no, bitch. When we leave here, I am following you to a CVS or Walgreens, and we will be getting you a pregnancy test, missy, before you go in the house!"

"I want a drink tonight though." I poked my bottom lip out.

"Only red wine and you're lucky I am going to let you get that. You're not about to be having my god child coming out of your pussy already on Pluto." She rolled her eyes.

We ordered our food, and I settled for some red merlot to drink. Quinn was scaring me but not enough for a little bit of alcohol. After dinner, Quinn ransacked CVS's feminine product section, loading up on the First Response pregnancy tests, and we went back to my place.

***

"Logan, has it been three minutes yet?" Quinn hollered to me while I sat on the toilet, staring at the test in my hand.

"No!" I lied. It read "Positive" before the three minutes were even up. I was sitting there trying to take in my reality. I had, had sharp pains and cramps in my lower abdomen on and off while we were in Miami, but I kept trying to ignore it. I heard her footsteps coming toward the bathroom door, and I tried shutting it, but I was too slow. She reached for the test in my hand, and she read it out loud.

"Positive!" she screamed and hugged me, rocking back and forth.

I was still in shock myself. I couldn't even respond back. I didn't know if I was happy or upset about it. I had to figure out a way to tell

Dre. *This nigga still hasn't called or been home today, come to think of it.*

"Dre is going to be so happy!" I finally mustered up myself to say.

"Yes, oh my goodness! I'm so excited! I can't wait to buy all the cute little outfits!"

"Well, it definitely explains why I've been feeling so off the last couple of weeks," I said.

"I still can't believe you kept this all from me, but for the sake of the baby, I will let you off the hook." She hit me on the shoulder then walked out of the bathroom.

I followed her in the living room. "I'm sorry, darling!"

She began gathering her belongings. "Now that, that's over with, I can go home to get ready for work in the morning. Enjoy your day off."

"Text me to let me know you're home safely." I walked her to the door.

"Bye, baby." She rubbed my belly and left out.

After closing the door behind her, I sat on the couch deep in my own thoughts. I decided to text Dre.

Me: U ok?

I never got a response. I hoped things were okay and he wasn't locked up or anything. I fell asleep and woke up around 4 a.m. and I realized I was still lying on the couch. I went into my bedroom and realized Dre still wasn't there. My mind started racing wondering where exactly he could be. I tried calling two of his phones, and they all just kept ringing. He still hadn't answered my text message back either. My mind was making me think he was out cheating. Which reminded me, I was the one who set up his iCloud email and password. So I went to the Find My iPhone app and put in his information. His location showed he was at some Motel 6 near the airport. Now, a part of me wanted to believe maybe he was doing business there, but the reality of the type of nigga I was dealing with set in quick. I hopped up and put on one of his t-shirts, my Victoria Secret sweatpants, and a pair of Nike Air max 95's. Before walking out of the door, I grabbed my gun and my brand-new pocket knife I bought from the gas station a few days ago, they were always handy. I hopped in my car quick, on a mission, and I was ready for whatever. *I don't like to be played with or fucked over, and Deandre knew better.*

I pulled up to the hotel and parked directly in front of his car. *This idiot had the balls to be parked front and center. He seemed to not even try to feel the need to hide.* I stepped out of my car and stood next to his passenger side. The tints on his Benz were so dark, I couldn't tell if someone was in there or not. I tried calling him one more time, and when he didn't answer, I sent him a picture of the pocketknife with his car showing in the background so he could see exactly where I was located. I bent down next to his tires and slashed three of them. I had once heard if all four tires were slashed on a car the person could claim insurance and have them reimburse the replacement tire cost. No, I didn't care how much money he had, I wanted for this nigga to be hurt and have to pay out of pocket for a brand-new set of tires. I bent back up quickly once I was satisfied with my handwork. I jumped back in my car I had left running, and when I was pulling out of the parking lot, I noticed him running out of a room toward my car. I sped off, damn near hitting him. Here I was just finding out I was pregnant with his child, and a few hours later, I had to deal with this stupid shit. On my way back home, Dre was blowing up my phone. I had gotten tired of hearing it blocking my music every time it would ring, so I turned it off so I could listen to my 90's slow jams in peace. *Fuck his bitch ass!*

I got home and went directly to the bedroom. I was feeling overwhelmed and began feeling nauseous. I jetted to the bathroom barely making it to the toilet. As soon as I was done, I jumped up feeling Dre's hand rubbing my upper back and shoulders.

"Logan! Look, I'm sorry. Ain't no shit go down, I had..."

"Fuck you, Dre! If I weren't feeling so weak right now, I would slap the shit out of you. Just leave me alone." I threw my clothes off and laid down in the bed.

It felt like I went directly to sleep, but I was awakened by my own heavy breathing and a euphoric feeling. When I mustered up the strength to open my eyes and look down, Dre's head was in between my legs. He was licking and sucking on my pussy better than he ever had, and all of the rest of the times, I thought was the best. Everything in my mind wanted me to push him off, but my flesh allowed for me to let him keep going. He pulled all of the rest of his clothes off and stuck his dick inside of me. I could tell the difference in my pussy since I've had the pregnancy symptoms. My shit was gushing, and I was always horny. Dre's dick slid in and out of me smooth like a glove, and I was feeling every stroke going in and out of me in a way that I had never felt before.

"Shit, Lo, your shit is extra wet!" Dre yelled.

"Ahhhh, Dre, don't slow down." I tried matching his rhythm.

"Shit, Lo, you gonna make me bust too quick." He slowed down and flipped me on my stomach and began hitting me from the back. He started speeding up, and neither one of us could take it anymore, we both bust prematurely together. We both were breathing hard. He laid back, and I laid on his chest.

"Lola Bunny, I'm sorry, baby!"

"How did you even get back here?"

"I drove on the flats all the way home. But my tires are run flats remember?" He smiled.

I laughed. "Shit, I wanted for you to be stranded."

"I can't drive on them but for so long before I have to get new tires."

"Dre, I found out I am really pregnant last night," I admitted.

He pulled me in even closer. "I already knew before you did. I'm excited as shit, this will be both of our first child! Big Rell is going to kill me though, shit!" He laughed.

I couldn't believe it. I didn't know what to think. Dre would have to get his shit together because I wouldn't raise a child in a bunch of mess. I may not have had the balls to tell my family about the bad shit he does, but I wasn't too scared to leave his ass with a child being involved. He thought I wouldn't be scared enough to leave him.

Apart of me felt like shit for pretty much letting him off with sex. It seemed like all of the values and morals I prided myself on, I was for some reason, now going against since I started dealing with Dre. I found myself not being able to think past my flesh anymore. My mind continued to race as I laid in his arms.

Dre

The next morning, I felt like shit honestly. Ashley was fucking my head up, and I had to get rid of this bitch. I got caught slipping with her up in the hotel room. I had to keep telling her to stay inside and hide in the bathroom. She kept talking about she was pregnant by me, but the dates weren't adding up, and the few times that I fucked her, I could've sworn we used condoms. I didn't plan on fucking her in the hotel room, I just told her to get a ride and meet me out there since I still had the room left from breaking down some work we had to catch up on. Me going to Miami had me running behind on my portion of the work outside of Dom, so I had some of the crew putting in overtime. That way, business would continue to be on overflow. I really didn't realize half the day was gone, and I hadn't talked to Lo. We wanted to keep our enemies guessing, and in order to do that, we had to move and bust down traps that weren't in well-known places but were still easily available to us. I knew Logan was pregnant before she even told me, her body was changing, not to mention how wet her pussy was. I wanted our baby more than anything. I needed to find a way to convince her to move to the house in Pennsylvania.

Today I knew I had a lot of making up to do. I told Logan to ride with me all day since she didn't have to go back to work until tomorrow. We went to raggedy ass Denny's for breakfast first.

I opened the door for her, and when she walked in, I couldn't help but to admire her ass and slap it.

"Stop, Dre!" She tried pouting.

"Stop complaining. I should be the one complaining, you got me up in here at dirty ass Denny's!"

"I had a taste for some good pancakes. You told me while I am pregnant I can have anything I want." I shook my head and the waitress bought over our orders.

We sat around eating and I noticed a familiar face in the booth across from us. It was the clown ass nigga my mother introduced me to the last time I was at her house. My mother knew not to introduce me to anybody that I didn't feel was good enough for her, but her old ass still only liked them Bud Ice sipping old men, which I hated. The old bitch he was chilling with damn sure wasn't my loud ass mother. I began getting heated. I called her while Logan was eyeing me the entire time, trying to figure out why my mood changed.

"Aye, Ma, what's that nigga name you introduced me to the other day?"

"Are you talking about Dave?"

"Yeah, that's him. Y'all still talk?"

"Yeah, what is going on, Dre Dre?" She sounded serious.

"Nothing, I'm about to whip his ass he up in Denny's with some ole ugly bitch," I said hanging up. Logan looked at me with her eyes wide open. I knew how scared she was when I got mad.

"No, no, Dre, calm down." She tried grabbing me as I got up

fuming. I kept walking past her, reaching the table Dave was sitting at.

"What's up, Dave?" He looked shocked.

"Hey, man, what's up, how you…" He began to speak, and Logan walked up beside me pulling on my shirt.

I didn't even give him a chance to finish his sentence before I yanked him up out of the booth by his collar.

"You fucking around on my mother, nigga!" I yelled, and the whole entire restaurant grew silent staring in our direction.

"Baby, no!" Logan yelled, but she knew it was no stopping me.

I dropped him down on the ground and punched him a few times in the face. I was moving too fast for him, he didn't know what hit him. I felt a pair of hands grabbing me. It must've been the restaurant manager, it was a tall white dude. I was so mad, I punched him in the face for even touching me.

"Dre, come on!" Logan screamed, walking quickly toward the exit.

She hopped in the driver's seat of my G-Wagon and sped off.

"Dre, I know you were mad, but baby, you could've been on your way to jail right now. We were already on our way to see your lawyer as it is. Baby, I love you, and now we have a child involved, we just have to be wiser with our decisions."

"I know, babe, but that nigga was foul as fuck in there," I said.

She pulled up to my lawyer's house, and we sat there for a minute in silence. I noticed she grabbed my hand and had begun to say a silent prayer for me with her eyes closed. *This was my wife.* We got out of the truck and walked hand in hand to his door. He was a short Jewish man that went by the name Po. Po was down for anything I told him, and I always told him the truth so he could come up with the right scheme to get me out of my situations in the right ways. The problem with my case was that Po could pay to get me off of the actual gun charge, but he was having a hard time with getting my racist ass probation officer not to violate me. They wanted me to sign an eight-year plea deal, and I wasn't having that shit. That's another reason I was on grind overload within the last couple days; my court date was coming up in a few. *Logan was going to leave my ass for sure.* I wasn't sure if the baby was going to hold her still and keep her around. She was too independent not to think rationally, like I didn't want her to do right now. I was a selfish nigga, and I wanted her by my side forever. I had to keep her distracted from everything.

CHAPTER 25

Logan

My heart was crushed when I heard Mr. Po say eight damn years. I knew I had to be strong for not only myself, but also my unborn child and Dre. A woman could only take but so much. I was having abdominal cramps really bad since last night, and I didn't want to tell Dre for him to want to rush me to the hospital every five minutes. I figured I had gotten pregnant from our night in Atlantic City. I set up a doctor's appointment for tomorrow after work. I think that was the only thing that made Dre sane for the rest of our day as we rode around handling business. We pulled up to one of his traps over east Baltimore, and before he got out, I grabbed his hand.

"Dre, maybe we should just go get married and secure our future, so at least that way we know we have one another after all this shit is over." I stared at him deeply in his eyes while he looked back at me speechless.

He shook his head. "Logan, you don't know what you're saying right now, you're just speaking from emotion," he said, letting my hand go and getting out of the car.

I felt crushed. His psyche was going down by the hour, and I didn't know what to do. I knew I was doing my part by showing him I would stand by him, but then he had the nerve to deny me. I sat back listening to music and rubbing my stomach. These sharp pains in my abdomen were beginning to get on my nerves, I couldn't wait for my doctor's appointment.

Minutes later, he hopped back in the car, counting a wad of money he pulled from out of a brown paper bag. My eyes began to water as I heard him counting, I couldn't help but to think about how much he allowed all of the money he was making to control his life and his emotions. *Money was his first love and not me, so when it's time for me to have this baby, will he do the same to our child?*

He looked up at me, breaking his concentration. "Lo Lo, are you crying?"

"Dre, you should be trying your best to become the man you want for your children to see you as!" I randomly yelled out.

He put the money away and got out of the passenger side, coming around to me, softly pulling me out of the car and kissed me on my forehead. "Come on, Lola Bunny, not right here. Get in on the other side, I will drive."

He watched me get in before he got in and drove off headed toward 295 southbound. I guess I was so emotional, I ended up falling asleep, and when I woke up, I noticed we were in D.C. pulling up at the District Chophouse & Brewery restaurant. He parallel parked a few blocks away. He got out and opened my door and gave me his hand to hold. We walked down the street hand in hand, and Dre kept trying to steal looks from me as we walked. I couldn't help but to glance back at him and laugh.

I shook my head at him. "Dre, you are so silly."

"Damn Lo, I got to deal with you and this emotional shit already." He laughed shaking his head.

"You sure as hell do!" I slapped him on his chest and laughed.

We went inside, and we were seated at a plush booth. Dre instantly grabbed both of my hands as soon as we sat down. He stared me in my eyes and blew a kiss at me, making me laugh at him. He was so corny at times, but I loved him for that.

"Dre, you are such a damn clown!" We both burst out laughing.

The waiter came over to take our orders, and the pain in my stomach started up again. I guess Dre noticed the change of emotion on my face.

"Lo, what's wrong?"

"Nothing, I'm just hungry that's all," I lied.

"You're always lying to me," he said.

"No I don't! Just leave it alone!" I snapped a bit. *This nigga never wanted me to lie to him like he always did me!*

The waiter came over with our drinks, just in time, breaking up whatever argument was about to transpire between us.

Dre

Logan never realized how in tune I was with her mind and body. She kept holding and rubbing her stomach like she was uncomfortable or something. I was going to leave it alone for now, but tomorrow at the doctor's appointment, I would get in her ass about it in front of the doctor. We ate our food and headed back to Baltimore. Dom text me while we were eating that I needed to come and meet him at the trap house over east ASAP. It was always a problem over there. I was going to drop Logan off at home and switch cars. When I made sure she was relaxed and okay, I decided to take my everyday S550 so I could get it washed while I was out. I never wanted for niggas to be able to recognize me in any other type of car.

On the way over there, Candi started blowing up my phone and texting me about how much she wanted me dead and shit. I just blocked her number. I wasn't worried about that bitch. She was just in her feelings and playing hurt. I pulled up on the block and spotted Dom. I got out, dapping him up.

"What's good, bro bro?" Dom said.

"Shit, getting to this money," I said.

"Everything is looking good with the money, but I feel like it's some eyes out here. For the evening, business is business, and the daily quota had been made an hour ago, but we need to ride out to Harford County to check on the newest shipment from Emilio."

"Say no more. Hop in with me."

We got in the car, and Dom wasted no time sparking his blunt he already had pre-rolled. We were the type of niggas to all always pay attention to our surroundings. I noticed Dom kept looking through the side mirror as we headed toward the highway.

"Aye, Dre, you notice that blue Honda coupe has been following us for the past five minutes?" Dom said.

As soon as those words left his mouth, I began to take notice and made a U-turn headed toward Pulaski highway to see if whoever it was would follow us. We had a car stash garage on each side of town, in case of emergencies, if any of us ever needed a low-key looking car to disguise ourselves in. The same car was still following us when we turned.

"Oh fuck no! Nigga, you got your strap on you?" I yelled pulling my heat out.

"You already know, nigga." Dom put his blunt down and pulled his gun out of his waist looking behind us.

A few seconds later, in the middle of traffic, gunshots came in our direction from the same car. I ducked down flooring it in the direction of the garage, and Dom jumped up with half his body outside of the passenger window firing back. One shot hit their front tires, and they lost control of the car and crashed into a light pole. After he let off a few more rounds in their direction, he sat back down inside the car.

"Nigga, who the fuck was they?" I asked.

"Fuck if I know. All I do know is if they knew who they was fucking with, they wouldn't have been dumb enough to pull a amateur ass move like that and think they would be able to live and tell it!" Dom's adrenaline was still pumping.

"Yo, who the fuck could that have been! This some bullshit!" I yelled hitting the steering wheel. My back window was shot out.

"Fuck whoever it was, we got them niggas. They'll show their faces again soon. All that matters is we are still alive, nigga, fuck it," Dom said sternly.

"You right, bro!"

We got to the garage and switched cars, leaving my Benz there until I felt like getting the window fixed. Dom ended up driving to Harford County to the spot, my head was fucked up. My life was beginning to go too far downhill at this point. I was feeling like I was losing control over every part of my life, and that feeling was fucking my head up. Logan didn't deserve this shit. As bad as it sounded, I knew I needed to leave her.

* * *

That night I got home, and Logan was knocked out curled up on her side. When I looked at her face, it looked like she had been crying again. The pillow was wet next to her face as well. I felt like shit even more because everything that was making her sad was because of me. She was really the love of my life, and I didn't honestly know how to love her back, but my pride wouldn't let me let her go. So I continued to drag her through the mud with me.

I took my clothes off and got in the shower. I had to sit there for a minute and think about everything that was going on. I knew one thing though; if I was really going to jail, I had to knock Ashley off before she would become a serious problem. I finished washing up and slid softly into the bed, pulling Logan close to me, kissing her on her shoulders. I always could tell how relaxed her body got when I was around.

Logan

I got up early to get ready for work. Dre was knocked out on his back snoring. *I hated to hear that shit!* I just shook my head and went in the bathroom to wash up and get ready. When I came out with my uniform on, Dre was still calling the cows, usually he would wake up after hearing me in the shower, but I decided to leave him alone, he must've had a long night. He'll just fill me in later.

I got to work and the first person I saw walking in was Derrick, who I hadn't seen in a few weeks. I had been avoiding him at all cost. Especially now that I was pregnant, I don't want him nagging me about going out or all in my business period. I made a quick turn into the bathroom before he could notice me. I watched him through the glass in the door as he walked by, and I was able to quickly head to my locker to put away my belongings. I needed to leave early today in order to make it to my doctor's appointment. Quinn and Kelsi made me put them on stand by for when I left the appointment because they just had to know all of the details.

By the time my lunch break came, I couldn't even concentrate on work because Dre wasn't answering the phone or my text. On the regular, he always worried me to death about contacting him throughout the day because he missed me so much, so this was a bit odd to me. *Fuck! I hope he didn't get locked up!*

By the time I got off, I was calling and texting, and his phone was now going straight to voicemail. This shit with always worrying about him all the time was really beginning to grind my fucking gears. This was the both of our first child, and here I am, having to hunt him down to go to a simple ass doctor's appointment. I drove toward the OBGYN's office and noticed a text from Malia.

Malia: Have you heard from Dre today? I think some shit went down

I was scared to even reply. I just looked at the message and set my phone back in the center console, shaking my head. Something was wrong, and at this supposed to be happy moment in my life, something else fucked up was obviously going on, and I didn't have the energy to confront it. Dre and I were so wrapped up in each other, we still had yet to sit our parents down to tell them we were expecting. Life was moving too fast, and I couldn't catch up anymore. We had finally become official and moved in together, yet, I was still feeling less than. While I was inside the office, I couldn't keep Dre off my mind. Everything the doctor was saying was going in one ear and out of the other. I took a blood test to verify my pregnancy, and she wrote a prescription for some type of specialized prenatal vitamins. She warned me that it seemed my stress level and sodium intake was too high already, which played a major role in my cramping fazes. I had to get myself together for the sake of the baby.

When I left, I texted Quinn and Kelsi to give them an update on how my appointment went. I didn't feel like talking to either one of them or anybody, for that matter. On my way in the house, I decided to stop at Chipotle to get something to eat. While I was in the long line, my mom was calling me, but I ignored her call too, and text her back.

Me: Mommy I will call you back when I get home from work.

Mommy: Ok baby love you.

Me: Love you too

I felt a bit bad for lying to her, but I was an emotional wreck at the moment. After I got my food, I headed back downtown toward my house. As I was driving, I prayed that God gave me patience this evening because him giving me strength would lead to me needing bail money tonight once I caught up with Dre.

I got home and purposely didn't valet my car and parked myself in the garage to see that neither of Dre's cars were there. I got an attitude all over again. I got upstairs in the condo, and a bad feeling began to come over me. I went in the kitchen to sit my food down and I noticed Dre's phone charger that he always kept there was gone. I stood a bit puzzled for a second. I decided to go in my closet to take my work clothes off and put something on a bit more relaxing. When I walked in, I saw that all of Dre's clothes and shoes were gone. I was crushed. I was so mad I couldn't even cry. *The nerve of this bitch ass nigga! I'm pregnant with his child, and he leaves me!* I changed and went back in the kitchen to eat my food. I heard my phone ringing hoping it was Dre calling, but I saw it was Quinn calling me.

"Hello!" I yelled.

"Damn, Lo Lo. What's wrong?"

"Dre's bitch ass is gone!"

"What the fuck you mean, Logan? You're pregnant!"

"I came home a few minutes ago, and all his shit is gone, and he's been ignoring my calls all day. He didn't even show up to my appointment," I said fighting back my tears.

"Oh fuck no! I am on my way!" She hung up.

This was my entire fault. I chose to overlook all of his disappointments. I felt like I was sinking. My world had turned completely upside down. I told myself I would never be with a guy that was in the game ever again, and now look what had happened. I am supposed to be focused on school and starting my business, not this bum ass shit.

* * *

Quinn ended up coming over about an hour later that night. She was such a good friend, she let me sit up all night and cry in her arms without me having to worry about her judging me. It took me a day to get myself together, but I was able to get myself up to go to work two days later, after the whole ordeal. All this pain over a man wasn't worth it.

It had been about three weeks, and I still hadn't talked to Dre, only God knew where he was. I'm sure he went back to his bitch. I wasn't feeling calling Malia or Dom to see what was up, because I'm sure Dom was down with whatever was going on and told Malia to keep it from me. I wasn't with the phony shit. I was on my way to Whole Foods after I got off this afternoon. I had my music blasting, jamming to Ball Greezy's song, "Nice & Slow," when my damn phone interrupted me in the middle of me winding my body in the seat at the red light. I was officially six weeks today, so I was in a good mood.

It was a number I didn't recognize, but it may have been my job, so I answered it.

"Hello?"

"You have a collect call from Deandre Johnson an inmate at a Maryland Correctional Facility. To answer this call press zero, to refuse this call, simply hang up. To block any future calls dial—"

I pressed zero so damn fast.

"Dre?"

"Lola Bunny. Hey, baby."

"Nigga, first of all, fuck you! I'm out here pregnant with your child, and you leave me high and dry!" I yelled.

"Nah, baby. It's not even like that. I had to get away. It's hella shit that went down. I need to see you ASAP, and how is the baby?"

"No, Dre. You need to be a man and be honest with yourself and confront all of your issues you keep running away from!" I yelled.

"Damn, Lo. You didn't have to say it like that."

"I'm out this bitch by myself, Dre. Fuck you!" I hung up.

I was so overwhelmed that I thought I was going to be able to get some type of satisfaction for telling him how I felt, but it did absolutely nothing but piss me off. My stomach started cramping up really bad, so I decided to just go home instead. By the time I was walking to the elevator in my building, I could barely walk. I was hoping none of my neighbors would be coming or going once the elevator stopped on my floor. I was holding my stomach so tight, scared that something was wrong. I was damn near crawling to my front door to open it so that

I could get inside. As I struggled to get my keys out, I felt something dripping down my leg, and I noticed blood was beginning to stain my work scrubs in between my legs. I finally got the door opened and tried my best to walk to my bathroom. Once I got inside the bathroom, I instantly fell on the floor. The pain was getting to be unbearable, and I was crying uncontrollably. I had to be having a miscarriage at this point. I must've been stressing too much since Dre left, I guess. I still had my phone in my hand, and I started to call my mom, when all of a sudden, I heard a hard knock on my door. When I didn't answer, they began knocking even harder like they were the police.

...TO BE CONTINUED

"Recklessly In Love With A B-More Thug 2" Coming soon!

ACKNOWLEDGEMENTS

First and foremost, I would like to thank God. Without Him and my savior Jesus Christ, I would not be where I am today. I thank God for revealing my purpose and strength most of all. I am blessed to have a great support system around me. My cousin/sister Farrin Hymon, of FARRINHEIT Entertainment & Media, we have been thick as thieves since birth. My best friends, Martitez Watkins and Nyasha Bivins; they have never turned their backs on me and have been my riders since day one. My good friend and big sister, Temi Roberts of Lady Styles Hair Designs; I love you dearly, and I thank God for you taking me under your wing after all these years. To my parents, Darnell and Sonja, I appreciate and love you both with everything in me. To the rest of my family and friends, I love you all dearly, and thanks for the support. To my baby dog, Nova the Shih Tzu, Mommy loves you. Thanks to my pen sister, Author Traci B, for giving me the motivation I needed and for having a listening ear from the beginning. And last but not least, thanks to Porscha Sterling, CEO of Royalty Publishing House, for taking a chance on me as a new author. I truly appreciate it. Much love and success to my entire Royalty Publishing House family of authors!

CONTACT AUTHOR BRIA S. ON

Facebook: *www.facebook.com/authorbrias*

www.facebook.com/ladee.bri

Instagram: *@ladee.bri*

Looking for a publishing home?

Royalty Publishing House, Where the Royals reside, is accepting submissions for writers in the urban fiction genre. If you're interested, submit the first 3-4 chapters with your synopsis to submissions@royaltypublishinghouse.com.

Check out our website for more information: www.royaltypublishinghouse.com.

Text ROYALTY to 42828 to join our mailing list!

To submit a manuscript for our review, email us at
submissions@royaltypublishinghouse.com

Text RPHCHRISTIAN to 22828 for our
CHRISTIAN ROMANCE novels!

Text RPHROMANCE to 22828 for our
INTERRACIAL ROMANCE novels!

Get LiT!

Download the LiT eReader app today and enjoy exclusive content, free books, and more

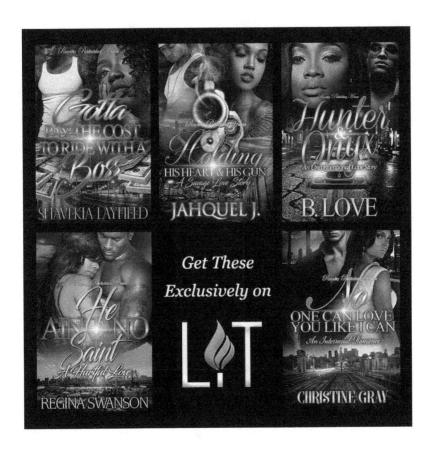

CPSIA information can be obtained
at www.ICGtesting.com
Printed in the USA
LVHW01s2302070618
579960LV00011B/1045/P